All Books by Harper Lin

The Patisserie Mysteries
Macaron Murder: Book 1
Éclair Murder: Book 2
Baguette Murder: Book 3
Crêpe Murder: Book 4
Croissant Murder: Book 5
Crème Brûlée Murder: Book 6
Madeleine Murder: Book 7

The Emma Wild Mysteries
4-Book Holiday Series
Killer Christmas: Book 1
New Year's Slay: Book 2
Death of a Snowman: Book 3
Valentine's Victim: Book 4

The Wonder Cats Mysteries
A Hiss-tory of Magic: Book 1

www.HarperLin.com

Macaron Murder

Harper Lin

A Patisserie Mystery
Book #1

ISBN-13: 978-0992027964

ISBN-10: 0992027969

Contents

Recipes

Chapter 1

Clémence Damour carried her travel backpack up the exit staircase of Métro Trocadéro. She faced the familiar bustle of the Parisian cafés brimming with locals and tourists alike while lanky waiters in white dress shirts and black vests served them with grim politeness. After spending more than twenty-one hours on a flight from Melbourne then riding the RER B train from Charles de Gaulle Airport, she felt exhausted and more than a little gross. She hadn't showered in two days and had slept terribly on the plane.

Australia had been her last stop after traveling the world for two years, and now she was back in her hometown of Paris, France. The posh sixteenth arrondissement hadn't always been her neighborhood. Her parents acquired their luxury three-bedroom apartment on the fifth floor of a Haussmannian building in one of Paris's most exclusive neighborhoods after she had graduated *lycée*, the French equivalent of high school. She had actually grown up in a humble house in the suburbs and wasn't used to the chic ladies in Chanel jackets with their Hermès bags and the dashing men in well-cut Armani suits.

Among the well coiffed and the well dressed now, she felt like a hobo with her unwashed hair, her grubby travel clothes, and her unfashionable backpack. People-watching was a popular Parisian pastime, and she could feel the eyes on her as she walked from the Métro exit to a nearby bench. They didn't know that she was the heiress to one of the country's most popular dessert and pastry chains.

It was strange to be back in Paris after all that she'd seen and experienced on her travels. She saw her surroundings with fresh eyes, as the snap-happy tourists would: the beautiful, uniform architecture; the cafés with the tiny tables barely big enough for one person, let alone two; the grand museums of the Palais de Chaillot etched with lines of poetry by Paul Valéry; the trees just beginning to bloom in the onset of spring. But her favorite view was the one directly across from Café du Trocadéro.

Her old friend, the iconic Eiffel Tower, stood strong and confident across the Seine River. Place du Trocadéro had the best viewing platform facing the tower, where ecstatic tourists gathered to pose for photos.

Clémence sat down on the bench to admire the view. Even though she was a French native, she never got tired of staring at her. The tower was female, as *La* Tour Eiffel used a feminine article.

La Tour stood so boldly, with such strength and conviction of her own beauty and power, that Clémence was inspired by her mere presence.

Whenever Clémence used to visit her parents' apartment, she would sit on the balcony, which also had a great view of La Tour, with a cup of tea. She could easily spend an afternoon staring and meditating as a way of unwinding.

She had really lived in the last two years of her life, but now that she was back, her travels felt like a long distraction from her Parisian life.

She sighed as she looked at her old friend now and spoke to her silently. *I'm back. Did you miss me? I guess it was time to come back to reality.*

Chapter 2

Clémence strolled to Avenue Kléber, noting and enjoying the beautiful architectural details on each building façade. She was in no hurry as no one was waiting for her at 14 Avenue Kléber except their dog Miffy, who had been left with a neighbor.

When Clémence had left for her travels two years ago, she also moved out of the apartment that she shared with her then-boyfriend Mathieu in Le Marais. Now that she was back, she would stay at her parents' place. It was near-perfect timing. The week before, the Damours had left for a travel adventure of their own. They would be living in Tokyo for six months and then Hong Kong, as they oversaw the opening of more Damour patisseries and tea salons in each city.

The original Damour patisserie was in the sixteenth arrondissement of Paris, right in the neighborhood where they lived now, which was why they had moved here from the suburbs to begin with. Her parents were both bakers. Her father was French, and her mother was American. They had met and fallen in love while attending a Parisian culinary school for pastry making, and then they went into business together after a shotgun wedding. Damour was how they made their fortune. What started out as a small neighborhood bakery selling classic French desserts with some American and international influences became a hit with the locals. They expanded to two more locations around Paris.

Damour quickly became a franchise. They now had locations around France, such as in Nice and Cannes. There was one in New York and one in London. Their packaged chocolates, candies, tea, and drink mixes were also sold in gourmet supermarkets around the world. The name "Damour" had become synonymous with gourmet desserts and treats.

Clémence loved the location in the sixteenth the most. It had started off as a regular patisserie with only a couple of tables because the shop was so small, but word soon spread, and it became so popular and crowded that they had to expand to a bigger location. It included a *salon de thé* as well, a tea salon where ladies could come for lunch, teenagers could hang out to do their homework, and people on the go could buy their favorite desserts to take home. It was a popular hangout for people of all ages, as the place was modern, clean, and "French" enough to be a classic brand but not so posh that people felt uncomfortable passing an afternoon there.

Apart from being her parents' house sitter and dog sitter for the next year, she would also help oversee the shops, particularly their flagship location in the sixteenth, which was a mere two-minute walk from where she lived. Clémence had gone to art school to be a painter, but she had grown up with a thorough knowledge of baking and desserts thanks to her parents. They were hoping that she would inherit the family business one day, along with her siblings, but she wasn't sure about making it a full-time career yet. She still had hopes of becoming a great painter someday.

When Clémence got to 14 Avenue Kléber, she saw la gardienne sweeping in the courtyard through the huge iron front door. She knew the code to get in, and she pushed the heavy door open. La gardienne was a stout lady in her late fifties, with mop-like white and gray hair and a bulbous nose.

When she heard Clémence coming in, she turned around and narrowed her eyes at her. "*Bonjour,*" she said roughly. "Can I help you?" From the way she scrutinized Clémence, it was as if she thought Clémence was some sort of unsavory vagrant or thief.

"*Bonjour*, madame. *Je suis* Clémence Damour."

"Ah." A knowing look began to spread in la gardienne's eyes, but she was still not smiling. "I didn't recognize you."

She gave her another disapproving once-over. It was true that Clémence didn't look her best, but she didn't appreciate the blatant rudeness of la gardienne's critical eye. Clémence couldn't wait to escape to her home.

La gardienne unlocked the door to her own apartment, which was just beside the front door, and disappeared inside.

She was the caretaker in charge of two buildings. These two buildings connected with another two buildings around a private courtyard. In each of the buildings, one apartment took up the entire floor. There were six floors in each building, plus the top floor that used to be the servants' quarters.

La gardienne lived on the ground floor, and she was in charge of delivering the mail, cleaning, overseeing who was coming and going, and handling small maintenance tasks around the building. It was in all the residents' favor to be on her good side.

Clémence didn't even know la gardienne's real name. Her parents had always just called her "la gardienne." She would have to ask them, but in a way, she didn't want to know. She couldn't imagine calling her anything other than "la gardienne."

The woman was moody, gruff, nosy, and a huge gossip. Everybody generally tried to stay out of her way—and her wrath. Clémence's parents complained to her about their run-ins with la gardienne so often that Clémence felt as if she already knew her well, even though she'd only seen her in passing when she used to come to visit her parents.

It was fun to hear anecdotes about la gardienne when Clémence had been out of the country, but now that she was living at 14 Avenue Kléber, she had to stay out of her hair to avoid getting trapped in conversations. La gardienne's negativity and complaints about the other residents, as well as general rants about life, could be draining. La gardienne didn't have a lot in life, aside from her job: no family, no great social life, not even good health—as she walked with a limp—and often complained to Clémence's mother about back problems.

When la gardienne came back out from her apartment, she held out something in her left hand.

"Here are the keys your parents left for you. This one is for the front door, this one is for the door of your building, and this one is for your apartment."

"*Merci beaucoup.*" Clémence put on her most pleasant smile.

She was glad that la gardienne didn't want to chitchat, as she apparently did with her mother. She seemed to be in a hurry to get back to her sweeping, so Clémence took her cue to go inside her building.

The tiny elevator, barely big enough for two people, took her up to the fifth floor. She unlocked the door and quickly punched in the code to deactivate the security alarm.

She dropped her backpack, and the first thing she did was open the windows to let the air and the light in. The main hallway had two shimmering chandeliers. The apartment was decorated in a hip, bourgeois way—classical paintings and baroque furniture mixed with chic modern furniture and abstract art. In the hall was a painting of a group of pink flamingos, which Clémence had painted at age nineteen and her parents had treasured enough to prominently display.

Even though the place smelled a little musty—nothing a little airing out wouldn't fix—it felt nice to be in that apartment. Everything was exactly the same. She would have the entire apartment to herself, which would take some getting used to after staying in hostels or sleeping on friends' couches for the past couple of years. It made her parents' place seem even bigger and grander than ever.

There was hardly anything to eat in the kitchen. Her parents had been gone for a week already, and their housekeeper wouldn't come until next Wednesday. It was only Thursday. There was some Camembert cheese, a bottle of pasteurized milk, and some boudin sausages, but no baguette, as it would have been rock hard after a couple of days anyway. In the pantry, she found a box of whole-wheat penne pasta. She boiled water to make pasta with pesto sauce and heated up a thick sausage in a frying pan.

After lunch, her discomfort from long periods of travel still remained. She went into her bathroom inside her classically decorated bedroom and drew a bath.

The chevron wood flooring squeaked as she walked, and she could hear a baby crying from the floor below and footsteps from above. The floors and walls in France were as thin as Band-Aids, but she preferred this now that she was living alone. If something were to happen to her, the neighbors would hear her screams.

Just before she could get into the bathtub, the home phone rang.

"*Allô, chérie?*" It was her mother. "You're home already?"

"*Oui, maman,*" Clémence replied. "I'm just a bit jet-lagged, but I'm going to take a bath."

"Try not to sleep. Keep awake for as long as possible, and you'll be back on schedule in no time. Did la gardienne give you trouble about the keys?"

"No, but she's not exactly enthusiastic to see me."

Although her mother was American, she'd lived in France for over thirty-three years. Her French was flawless, and she was as sophisticated as any of the mothers of Clémence's friends.

"She's a pain in the derrière, but give her a box of macarons from the shop to be in her good graces. She has eyes and ears all over the place, you know."

"Oh, I'll be all right," Clémence said. "She doesn't scare me."

"It doesn't hurt to give her the macarons. She adores the stuff, especially from our store. She'll be as happy as a clam. Once we gave her a box of thirty-two just before your father's birthday party, and she gave us no trouble about the guests coming in and out all night."

"I'll be sure to do that," Clémence said. "Are you still in Tokyo?"

"Yes, and they don't have street names here, can you believe that? It's a system where they don't use street names but something to do with blocks and numbers. I don't get it."

"Oh, I remember. I got totally lost once, and none of the locals knew how to use my map either."

"So how do people find where they want to go?" her mother asked.

"They use their phones, or from memory, I guess."

"*C'est très bizarre.* Are you enjoying yourself back in Paris?"

"Sure. I mean, as soon as I get some rest. What about you?"

"It's simply mad here, but your father is loving every second. He's out buying some takeout noodles right now. I don't know why he doesn't just call room service. I suppose he wants to feel like a local. What do you recommend we do next?"

"Have you been in their Metro?" Clémence asked. "There are professional people pushers to push you on certain trains during rush hour. Imagine, getting crammed like sardines."

"It's not that much different from Paris," her mother said. "We haven't taken the Tokyo Metro yet. We take taxis everywhere. Otherwise, we'd get completely lost! Oh, the store opening was incredible. People lined up around the block, and the tea salon was booked for a month in advance."

"That's great, *maman*. I knew it would do well. I'll have to come once I get my bearings."

"Well, I don't want to keep you from your bath. Enjoy yourself, and don't forget Miffy. Magda comes on Wednesdays at two p.m. to clean, and we don't give her a key, so you'll have to be home at that time to let her in. You're going to the patisserie later?"

"Yes, I'll check in and introduce myself in case any of the staff has forgotten me."

"How can they? You're unforgettable. Well, call me if you get in any trouble."

"Give papa a *gros bisou* for me," Clémence said. "Bye."

Clémence soaked in the bath for a good half hour. In no time, the water was gray with soapsuds and her own filth. She had to draw another short bath to feel completely clean.

Even though she was home, she still hadn't made it official yet. There were friends and relatives scattered around the country whom she would have to reconnect with soon. There was also the staff at the bakery to integrate back into. She was officially the boss, but she wasn't the type to do the bossing around. There were already two managers for that. She was planning on being a regular in the back kitchen, where she'd whip up new desserts with her team.

Then there was her life to figure out, the direction she should take with her art. She'd done some charcoal sketches here and there during her travels, but she hadn't painted at all.

And she didn't even want to get started on her love life, which was nonexistent. There was a handsome Spanish fellow who had traveled with her and her friends for a couple of weeks, but long story short, he left as quickly as he had appeared.

She'd left home at twenty-six, and she was twenty-eight now. She'd grown up after all that she'd seen and done, but there was still a lot of growing up to do.

After soaking for another half an hour, she felt a lot more refreshed. She combed out her black bob and put on skinny jeans, a silk lavender top, and penny loafers, which instantly transformed her into looking the part of a chic young bourgeoise. It was amazing what a good scrubbing and some nice clothes could do for a woman—or anybody for that matter.

Clémence spritzed on her favorite Chanel perfume, and she was on her way. It was almost 4:00 p.m. She would take her mother's advice about not napping. Plus she couldn't wait to visit Damour. She was craving a good French macaron, something she'd been deprived of except when her family brought some for her when they visited her on various occasions in different parts of the world. A good chocolate macaron could make her day.

Chapter 3

The staff at Damour hadn't changed much except for three new hires, as her parents had informed her. The flagship patisserie was at 4 Place du Trocadéro, where it had a view of the Eiffel Tower. One door opened directly into the patisserie section and the other into the tea salon, although both sections were connected on the inside. It just made it easier for the customers to get into two lineups, and at certain times, especially on Saturdays at lunchtime, people could line up for up to an hour to get a seat in the salon.

It wasn't so busy on a Thursday afternoon, except for the bakery, so Clémence went in through the salon door. The hostess, Celine, greeted her.

"Clémence, c'est toi! You're finally back!"

Celine gave her a kiss on each cheek. They were around the same age, and they had been pretty good friends ever since Celine started working there three years ago. They had kept in touch by email when Clémence was away. Sometimes Celine would fill her in on the gossip among the staff or funny anecdotes about store regulars.

After catching up a little, Celine introduced her to the wait staff who were there, Pierre and Christine. Then there were the cashiers in the patisserie section, Marie and Raoul. Caroline, the manager that day, who was a friendly middle-aged woman with dark-blond ringlets, came out to greet her.

Pierre and Marie were new, but they both seemed very friendly. Clémence's parents were very particular about who they hired—they only wanted people who were happy to work there. Paris had a bad reputation for poor customer service, and they wanted no part in that at Damour, which was partly what made the place so popular.

The inside of the place was the same aesthetic as her house: a mixture of classic baroque and modern contemporary. It had her mother's influence all over it. There were chandeliers and floral porcelain teacups, and modern tables and chairs cut from clear plastic. Her mother really had a great eye. She had also overseen the branding, which used lavender packaging with a gold logo. The walls of the store were painted in lavender and other pastel colors.

The back kitchen was Clémence's favorite place. She loved watching the pastries getting made. She was a mean baker herself, but she was out of practice. The chefs and bakers greeted her kindly. Sebastien Soulier was their star baker. He had been only an apprentice when Clémence first met him years back, but he'd recently been promoted to head baker.

"*Salut*, Sebastien. It's been a while."

Clémence gave him two kisses on the cheeks. Sebastien's younger sister, Berenice, was also working that day, and she greeted Clémence warmly with *bisous* as well.

Sebastien was making the shells for pistachio macarons, piping the pale-green mix onto a baking tray in one-inch circles. In an American twist—her mother's invention—this one had Oreo-flavored cream filling. It was absolutely delectable.

The Soulier brother and sister were both young and innovative as well. It was the reason why her parents hired them. Both had strawberry-blond hair, which could be categorized as red under direct sunlight, and flawless skin. Sebastien's eyes were hazel, while Berenice's were green. Clémence liked them both a lot.

"So glad you're back," Berenice said. "We'll have an extra hand in the kitchen again."

"Plus an extra tongue," Sebastien said. The girls gave him a funny look. "For taste testing. Get your minds out of the gutter. Clémence can help us with our new inventions."

Clémence picked a couple of fresh macarons from a tray and began munching. *Miam*. It was too good.

"I have some ideas of my own," Clémence said. "I've spent a good amount of time in Asia. How about an Asian-inspired line of macarons for this summer? I'm thinking green tea, red bean, lychee."

"Good idea," Berenice said. "Maybe cherry blossom too."

"We can get started right away," Clémence said. "Tomorrow, that is. I'm still not in the headspace."

"Don't worry," Sebastien said. "You have plenty of time."

Clémence stifled a yawn. "Suddenly, I'm feeling so drowsy. Maybe I should take a nap."

"Maybe you can sleep really early and wake up early," Berenice said.

"I've never been a morning person," Clémence said. "But maybe this is a perfect time to start."

Before she left, she got a box of sixteen macarons for la gardienne. Her mother had mentioned that she liked the pistachio-and-chocolate ones the most, so she selected four of them along with the usual chocolate, vanilla, and raspberry, and some Damour inventions, such as a cheesecake-flavored one, a s'more macaron, and even an olive oil and mint combo, which tasted better than it sounded.

She also got a box for the Dubois family, as they had taken care of Miffy for the past week.

The macarons were packaged in special collector's item boxes. She chose a chic zebra-pattern one for la gardienne and one patterned with little lipstick kisses for the Dubois family. Each came with a lavender bag with the store's gold logo.

She felt a lot better after reconnecting with her staff. Her parents were away, and the staff were the closest thing to family. She did have an aunt and uncle who had property in Montmartre, but they usually lived in Dubai. May was a month when many Parisians went away due to the various religious holidays. It was why some of the staff were away and the shop wasn't as bustling as it was normally.

La gardienne was inside her apartment when Clémence got home. She could hear la gardienne's TV through the door.

"Madame?" Clémence knocked.

There was no response, and Clémence tried again, knocking harder.

"Oui?" La gardienne opened the door so suddenly that Clémence almost jumped back.

La gardienne wore a sour expression, and the nostrils of her bulbous nose flared.

"I didn't mean to disturb you," Clémence said. "I just wanted to thank you for giving me the keys. Maman told me how much you love our macarons."

Clémence handed her the bag. La gardienne's expression seemed to soften... just a little.

"*Merci*," she said.

Clémence could tell that she still wasn't thrilled about her. She tried not to take it personally, as la gardienne apparently didn't like anyone, really. After she slammed the door shut, a dismissed Clémence went to the third floor.

A housekeeper opened the door. She showed her into the living room, where Madame Dubois was sitting with a café and a copy of *L'Officiel* magazine. She was an elegant brunette in her late fifties with tanned, leathery skin and a thin frame. She wore a navy-blue pencil skirt, a pink cardigan, and pearls around her neck.

"Ah, Clémence. Nice to see you again. Would you like something to drink?"

They gave each other *bisous* on the cheeks. Only a few hours back in Paris, and she'd kissed more people than she had in the two years she'd spent traveling. She had mostly traveled with American friends, who were accustomed to shaking hands, hugging, or nothing at all.

A little white dog, a West Highland terrier, came running up to her. Miffy! She jumped up Clémence's legs, her tongue out and tail wagging.

"I've missed you too, girl!" Clémence kissed Miffy on top of her head.

A couple of boys ran into the living room after Miffy. The Duboises were a large family. They were Catholic. There were seven kids in all, the oldest son being Clémence's age and the youngest son being seven. There were five boys and two girls in the family. The younger sets seemed to be troublemakers, and the older ones were taciturn and snotty. Clémence had only ever talked to Madame Dubois, as she was the friendliest out of the whole bunch.

The oldest son, Arthur, poked his head in. He had his own dog on a leash, a Jack Russell terrier with a red handkerchief tied around its neck.

"*Salut*," Clémence said.

Arthur gave her a stiff "*bonjour*."

"Clémence is house-sitting for the year," Madame Dubois said to her son. "So you'll be seeing a lot of her. Arthur has been the one walking the dogs this week."

"Thanks so much," Clémence said.

"No problem." Arthur backed away. "Well, I'm off."

Arthur was tall and dark haired. He would've been handsome if he smiled more and wasn't a complete snob. He had always rubbed Clémence the wrong way, and she hated his pink dress shirts and preppy cashmere sweaters that her American friends probably would've ridiculed. He wore the sweaters tied around his neck sometimes like a typical bourgeois guy.

A couple of times when Clémence had come to visit her parents for Sunday brunch, she'd seen Arthur coming out the side of the building with a different girl each time: good-looking girls in tight clothes and heels, doing the walk of shame.

Arthur didn't bring them home to his parents' house with all his siblings, of course. He had his own room on the top floor. In these Haussmannian buildings, the servants used to live on the top floor, because back then there were no elevators. To reach the top floor, one had to take a separate staircase, a harrowing, dingy one accessible through a small door beside the grand entrance door of the "real" apartments. The staircase took you directly to the top floor although, on each floor, it was connected to the kitchens of the main apartments.

Each apartment came with two or three servant rooms—*chambres de bonne*, as they were called. Some were bigger than others. Most were just a bedroom with a kitchenette. Two toilets were shared between the tenants on the floor, as well as a shower. Some rooms already had a toilet, a shower, or both. It was odd, but that was the way things worked.

Arthur was too old to be living at home, but he didn't want to part with the luxuries of doing so. He and his brother each took a servant's room, where they were free to commit whatever debauchery they wanted.

The Damours also owned two servant rooms. One was so small, and windowless as well, that they thought it was inhumane to allow anyone to live in it, so they used it for storage. Another room was a bit more spacious. It had a window with a view of the beautiful rooftops of Paris and a small shower next to the tiny kitchenette. Tenants changed from time to time, but right now, they had a British guy living there whom Clémence hadn't met yet.

The rent for these rooms was extremely cheap compared to the rent for a proper apartment. The other tenants were nannies, cleaners, or students. The rooms were practically dorm rooms. Arthur, however, had a housekeeper to clean up after him, and he went home for all his meals since the family employed a chef.

Clémence could tell that Madame Dubois wanted Arthur to pay more attention to Clémence. In the past, she had tried to coax Clémence's mother to set them up, but it wasn't happening. Clémence and

Arthur were like oil and water. She just hoped that he had been good to Miffy while they were away.

"So glad to have you back, girl." Clémence stroked Miffy's ears. She was beyond happy. With Miffy, the big apartment wouldn't feel so empty.

Chapter 4

Somebody was knocking on the kitchen door of the apartment. Clémence had been on the balcony, drinking her tea and having a silent chat with La Tour, when she went back inside the kitchen and heard it.

"Who is it?"

"It's Ben. From upstairs?"

He spoke English with a British accent. Clémence could tell the difference between British and American accents because she'd gone to university in America. Thanks to her mother, Clémence's English was nearly accentless. Sometimes, however, when she was tired, the French accent slipped through a little.

Clémence unlocked the door and opened up. A lanky guy with dark hair and dressed all in black–black V-neck tee and black jeans–stood in the staircase with a mischievous smile.

"You're Clémence, right? Hi, I'm Ben Mason. I wouldn't be bothering you this early except that I saw you from my window."

His room on the roof could see down into part of the kitchen.

"I'll be sure to wave next time I see you at the window," Clémence said.

They made their introductions, and Clémence let him in. Her parents liked Ben. He had finished his studies in English lit in Cambridge and was in Paris for the year to finish writing his novel. He also wrote poetry and went to open mics and writing workshops at the Shakespeare and Co. bookstore. Living in Paris was every writer's dream.

"Would you like a café?" Clémence asked, referring to the shots of espresso that the French preferred.

"That's okay," Ben said. "I've already had two cups."

"You're an early riser."

"I'm also a night owl. So I'm really an insomniac," he joked. "You rise pretty early yourself."

"I'm just jet-lagged, actually. Not really a natural early riser, but I'm hoping to stick with this schedule."

He peered at Clémence more closely. She blushed, wondering what the heck he was staring at.

"This is incredibly odd," he said.

"What?"

"I've spent so much time looking at your parents, and you look like an exact combination of the both of them."

Clémence laughed.

It was true that Clémence had her mother's dark hair and bone structure and her father's blue eyes and full lips.

"They talk about you a lot," Ben said. "Naturally."

She only hoped that they hadn't said anything too embarrassing.

"They told me about you, too," she said. "You're writing a novel? That's interesting. What's it about?"

"Well, I hate to call it a crime novel because it's more literary. So it's a literary crime novel, then. A man gets killed in the Tuileries, and he has a suitcase full of codes. The inspector has to figure out what it all means."

"Well, are you going to tell me?" Clémence asked.

"Actually, that's all I have so far. I'm hoping the rest of the plot will come to me soon."

Clémence laughed again. With Miffy and Ben around, she was feeling more at ease at home now. She had hoped that she and Ben could be friends, and things were looking good.

"Hey, I was wondering if I could get the number of your plumber," Ben said. "You see, my tiny sink is clogged. It's my fault for not pouring those chemicals as often as I probably should have. I should've listened to your mother."

"Please don't tell her that," Clémence joked. "So it's completely blocked?"

"Yes," Ben said. "I can't wash my hands anymore, so I need to do it in the shower."

"Oh gosh, sure. Actually, let's call him right now."

Clémence had the plumber's number on the home phone's directory. Luckily, the plumber was able to come in that morning but was very vague about the time. She gave the plumber Ben's cell phone number, as well as her own.

"Will you be at home all morning?" Clémence asked Ben when she hung up.

"Yes, I'll be writing."

"Great. Because I have to walk the dog, buy groceries, so I'll be in and out all morning. He'll call you when he's around."

"Thanks, Clémence," Ben said. "I'll see you soon. Oh, there's a poetry slam tomorrow night, and I'll be performing. Do you want to come? Bring some friends if you want."

"That sounds like fun," Clémence said. "Why not?"

"Great, I'll text you the details."

When Ben left, Clémence took Miffy out. She wanted to go all the way across the Seine to Champs de Mars, the park beneath the Eiffel Tower.

On her way out, she planned to tell la gardienne that a plumber was coming so that she wouldn't give him any trouble. She had a reputation for treating any intruders with rudeness and suspicion.

Her door was slightly ajar, and the TV was off, so Clémence knocked. When her phone rang, Clémence reached into her purse, loosening her grasp on Miffy's leash. Before she could get her phone, Miffy was off. She ran straight into la gardienne's apartment, pushing the door wide open.

"Miffy, no!"

Clémence went in after her.

"I'm sorry, madame—"

Then Clémence saw her: la gardienne on the floor with a pool of blood pouring from underneath her head.

Clémence screamed.

Miffy was barking and running around.

"No, Miffy, let's get out of here!"

Across from the apartment was a doctor's office. After Clémence banged on the door, the receptionist and some of the people in the waiting room came out.

"What's wrong?" asked the receptionist.

"Call the police!" Clémence exclaimed. "La gardienne is dead!"

Chapter 5

"Miffy, no!"

Miffy kept wanting to go back inside to look at the dead body, and Clémence had run to block the door.

"Please contain your dog, mademoiselle."

Cyril St. Clair, the inspector, managed to grab Miffy by the leash. He handed the leash back to Clémence. He was a man in his late thirties with smile lines like parentheses on the sides of his mouth. Not that he smiled much. It was when he grimaced that the lines appeared. He had a strong, hawk-like nose and intense green eyes that turned cold when they met Clémence's.

"Now, what is your name?" he asked.

"Clémence Damour."

"Damour?" He squinted at her. "You mean, of the Damour bakery chain?"

"Yes."

Cyril looked back down to his notepad and scribbled quickly.

"I see. Now tell me what happened."

Clémence explained that she was just trying to tell la gardienne that a plumber was coming by later that morning, but she found her body on the floor after Miffy ran in.

"It's rather a coincidence, then, that the victim had a box of macarons from your store, and she was in the middle of eating the macarons before she died?"

Clémence was taken aback by the blunt accusation.

"It is." Clémence told him that she had given her the macarons as a gift the day before.

"So it's also a coincidence that you happened to have found her dead this morning?"

"Yes," Clémence said with impatience. "I didn't find her exactly. As I told you, my dog ran in, and I ran in after her."

"You've messed up our investigation," Cyril said indignantly. "Your dog might have destroyed possible evidence."

As if on cue, Miffy spat out a button. A big wooden button.

Cyril made a disgusted face and picked up the button with only a thumb and an index finger.

"Any idea where this is from?" He looked at Clémence's outfit. She was wearing a black blazer and skinny jeans.

"It's not from any of my clothes," Clémence said.

Cyril sighed. "See, this is what I mean. It could've helped to have known whether the button was taken from la gardienne's apartment. And we could've checked for fingerprints."

Clémence couldn't help but roll her eyes. "Oh, please. If it wasn't for Miffy, you wouldn't even have an investigation so soon. She was the one who went in."

"Did anyone else see her go in?" Cyril raised an eyebrow.

"No, but I swear the door was open."

"And where were you last night?"

"I was home, sleeping. I just came back from Australia actually, and I was jet-lagged–"

"Who else lives with you?"

"With me? No one. It's my parents' apartment, and they're away."

"So let me get this straight. You live alone, and you don't have an alibi for last night. The victim had been eating a box of macarons that you gave her before she was murdered, and you just happened to find her dead in her apartment this morning."

"Yes." Clémence was exasperated already. She was starting to think this inspector was as dimwitted as the rest of the useless police in the city. If she were in his shoes, she'd take a closer look at the button. She would've found it curious that there were two drinking glasses on the table and one had a lipstick stain on it when la gardienne didn't wear lipstick. She would've taken a closer look at whatever it was that was written on the pad of paper on the table—everything except accuse an innocent person of murder.

But maybe she wasn't looking at this objectively. If she wasn't so offended by being accused of murder, she could see how Cyril would find her suspect.

But Clémence was no inspector. She wanted no part in this murder. And she certainly hadn't done anything wrong.

"If I was the killer," Clémence said, "which I'm not, why would I want to place myself in the position of finding her? Wouldn't I want to get as far away from the scene as possible?"

"It could be the work of a clever girl who thinks she can outwit a professional." Cyril looked at her smugly. "Finding her, screaming, acting innocent and clueless—I don't buy it."

"Look, I've told you all you need to know," Clémence said. "Why would I want to hurt la gardienne? I didn't even live here before yesterday. She's not very well liked by the rest of the residents. Maybe you can start questioning others who have actually interacted with her more than I have."

Cyril was still looking at her closely. "I'm not letting you off the hook yet, Clémence Damour, even if your patisserie does have the best almond croissant in the neighborhood."

"You mean 'in the world,'" Clémence said. "That reminds me, I have to go to the patisserie now, so if you'll excuse me, I'm off."

"Oh, wow," Berenice exclaimed in the kitchen. "A murder in your own building. Is it total chaos on your street right now?"

Clémence sighed. "Yes. The sidewalk has been taped off. Residents are scared. There were a million policemen and *pompiers* at the building even though she's already dead."

"You would've thought that the pope died or something," Sebastien quipped.

"And now this inspector thinks I'm involved."

She explained just what he had accused her of and the apparent evidence against her.

"It doesn't sound good," Sebastien said. He was in the middle of making an extravagant type of delicate raspberry tart that Marie Antoinette would have eaten in the Versailles Palace. "You really don't have an alibi?"

"Well, I was over on the third floor before I went home, but that had only been around six p.m. I was picking up our dog from a neighbor. Oh, but maybe the neighbors heard me walking when I was home. You know how thin the floors are. But I fell asleep at eight p.m. and was asleep for like twelve hours because I was so jet-legged. God, I really hope I'm not in trouble."

"It's like a *policier*," Berenice said.

"You like crime novels?" Clémence asked.

"Love them. I read crime and mystery all the time. There's a better way of trying to clear your name: find the killer."

"How would I do that? Besides, the smug inspector is on this case."

Berenice rolled her eyes. "Oh please, he's all talk. He was probably acting superior because he has no clue how to proceed. You know how Frenchmen are. They're like insecure little boys who need to act arrogant to mask their insecurities."

"Hey!" Sebastien exclaimed. "Or some of us are just talented and know it."

Clémence and Berenice both looked at him and looked back at each other. They tried not to roll their eyes.

"You're whip smart," Berenice said to Clémence. "I bet you can find the killer before the inspector does."

"I think you're overestimating me," Clémence said.

"Come on, you graduated from one of the best universities in France, you've traveled, and you always know what ingredients are in our macarons when Sebastien comes up with new recipes."

"Having good taste buds doesn't mean I'd be good at finding murderers," Clémence said.

"That's exactly what it means," Berenice said seriously. "It means your senses are heightened. Now, who do you think the suspects are?"

"I have no idea," Clémence said. "I hardly know who the neighbors are. There's a dentist on the first floor; that I know. Not sure who's on the second. The Dubois family lives on the third, but they couldn't have had anything to do with it. I have a tenant on the roof, and he seems really nice too."

"Who cares about nice?" Berenice said. "Murderers aren't going to walk around wearing a sign that says 'murderer.'"

"I'll let the police do the job," Clémence said. "What do I know about solving crimes?"

"You already noticed a bunch of clues. Take, for example, the lipstick on the glass. Would la gardienne even wear lipstick?"

"No, never. At least, I'd never seen her wear any sort of makeup. And it looked like this deep plum color that most women probably wouldn't even be able to pull off, either."

"There you go. That's something to start with. And you mentioned a button. What do you think it belonged to?"

"Well, it was a big wooden button, the kind that would be on a coat. It was so big that Miffy couldn't swallow it, which was probably why she spat it out. It could be nothing. Maybe la gardienne just had a coat, and the button fell off. I can't know unless I go in her apartment and look in her closet."

"And what about this paper?"

"Yes, there was a box of macarons on the table, and I guess she was snacking while writing something. But I saw the table only briefly before I noticed her body on the floor, so I didn't exactly read what the paper said, and I didn't care to. I suppose all these things are clues, but it could go nowhere. The lipstick stain on the glass could've been from a friend of hers who came in earlier to have a drink. For all I know, the murderer could be an outsider, a stranger, like a robber."

"But the person specifically went into la gardienne's apartment." Sebastien looked up from his work. "They wouldn't have much to steal. Was there a sign of forced entry?"

Clémence was surprised that Sebastien was taking an interest too. It didn't even seem as if he had been listening all that much, since he had looked as though he was in such deep concentration with his work.

"No. The door was just half open. The doorknob didn't look tampered with."

"The killer must've just fled in fear after killing la gardienne," Berenice said.

"It seems more likely that it would be someone who knows her," Sebastien said. "Maybe you can find out more about la gardienne and who hated her."

Clémence looked from brother to sister. They were both interested in this case. Pastries and mysteries—what an unusual combination! But she had to admit that she was curious. Who would do this and why? There were plenty of suspects in the building. Too many.

Clémence got a call on her cell phone. The display showed a number she didn't recognize. She answered it, and it was the plumber saying that he was at her front door, but the police weren't letting him in.

"Oh, crap." Clémence got up from her stool. "I've got to go deal with something. My plumber's trying to get in, and I might have to see that lame inspector again."

Chapter 6

When Clémence went back home, there were three policemen blocking the front door.

"*J'habite ici*," Clémence told them. "I live here."

The policemen asked her all sorts of questions, but after verifying that she did live on the fifth floor and she had the keys, they went in first to ask their superiors for permission to let her in.

The plumber had been standing on the sidewalk. Clémence didn't recognize him, as she'd never met him before, until she saw his bag of tools. Ben came out to meet them.

"Hey," he said to Clémence, his brows knitted with concern. "Good. You're here. He was having trouble coming in, so I came down to pick him up. What's going on out here? They wouldn't tell me."

Clémence explained that there had been a murder in the building, and both men's eyes widened in shock.

"*Mon dieu*," the plumber exclaimed.

"That's horrible," Ben said. "I mean, I know her—not well—but she was someone I saw on a regular basis. I've never met someone who was murdered before. That's something that happens on TV."

Clémence suppressed a sigh. She'd only been back a day, and so much was going on. Plus, she still had a bit of a headache from her jet lag and from sleeping too much.

"Come on, guys, let's go." Clémence turned to the plumber. "We can take the elevator and go through my apartment so that you don't have to climb all the stairs to the seventh floor with all your tools."

"It's good exercise, though," Ben joked. "I mean, it's how I keep this body in such top physical condition."

"I'm sure," Clémence said dryly. "Seriously though, if you ever have a lot of stuff to carry, don't hesitate to ring and pass by if I'm home."

"Thanks, that's nice. Your parents allowed me to do the same, but I tried not to bother them unless I had a suitcase or something. The fridge is so small that I never have a lot of groceries to carry anyway."

It was typical for people to live in tiny studio apartments or "studettes" like Ben's. His fridge was really a minifridge, and the sink could barely fit two plates. Clémence was lucky to be able to live in such a great apartment, even if it felt too big at times and their gardienne was currently, well, dead as a doorknob.

The inspector with the buggy green eyes and parentheses smirk came out of la gardienne's apartment just as she stepped through the iron door.

"Ah, it's *la heiress*," Cyril said. "Here with your goons?"

"Look, there's no need to be rude," Clémence said. "He's a plumber who's been waiting outside, and I had to come back from work just to let your men know that it's all right."

"Oh, I'm sorry that it's rather an inconvenience to you," Cyril said sarcastically, "but we're in the middle of a very important murder investigation, and we can't just let anyone in the building."

"How's that going, by the way?" Clémence was unable to keep the snark from her voice. "Find any leads yet?"

"Yes, plenty."

But Clémence could tell by his agitated expression that they had found very little.

"You know the button in Miffy's mouth?" Clémence asked. "Did you find a coat with a wooden button in la gardienne's house?"

"The button. No. La gardienne has no such coat. Which is why I say that it could've been a pivotal clue. Now I doubt the button is going to come back with anything concrete with your little dog's slobber all over it."

"Surely there are other things you must've picked up on," Clémence said. "What about—"

"Oh, mademoiselle," Cyril said. "Please let the professionals handle it. I think you've interfered enough. I'm still looking at you as our main suspect, and I don't need you tossing me any red herrings to throw me off your trail. You do need to come into the station to give your statement, so come in at three-thirty this afternoon."

Clémence fumed, but she held her tongue. Her temper had caused her trouble in the past, but she was a grown woman now. She didn't want some incompetent inspector to provoke her as though they were both ten-year-olds in a playground. He gave her a card with the address of the *prefecture de police*, and Clémence snatched it.

"Fine," Clémence said.

She went into her building, and Ben and the plumber followed.

"What a jerk," Ben said in English.

"You're telling me," Clémence replied.

The tiny elevator could fit only two people, and Ben offered to walk up because he was used to it. Five floors was nothing for him.

The elevator didn't go to the seventh floor. They had to pass through her apartment and go up the servant staircase. The top floor was less glamorous than the rest of the building. The hallway had no chic wallpaper and no chandeliers as the rest of the building. Fluorescent lights were used instead.

There was a room with a toilet in the hall that some of the tenants had to share. It greeted them when they rounded the staircase. The tiny, sinkless toilet room had a window, and whenever someone did their business, they were treated with a view of La Tour.

Ben unlocked the door to his little room.

On his table was a rusty blue typewriter, which he had been using that morning, judging by the half page already written, protruding from the top. A full ashtray of cigarette butts was beside it, along with novels and papers scattered all over the table. On the couch was a guitar. Empty glasses, beer bottles, and bags of chips were on the small kitchen counter, leaving no space for anything.

Ben rubbed the back of his neck out of embarrassment.

"Now that I'm looking at this room through your eyes, I see how messy it is."

"No worries," Clémence said with a smile. "You're a grown man. You can do what you want in your own room. Except let your sink get blocked, of course."

The plumber was already at work, and he found the problem. Using a long snake coil, he managed to get some pieces of food out of the pipes. The sink drained.

The smell from the water was horrible, and Clémence plugged her nose.

"Thank God," Ben said. "Now I can stop doing the dishes in the shower."

Clémence reached into her wallet to pay the plumber, but Ben insisted on paying. She knew that he was still paying off his student loans, so she turned down his offer.

"No, it's okay," Clémence said. "You're our tenant. We'll take care of it."

"But I was the one who caused the problem to begin with."

"Tell you what—if it happens again, you can pay the full amount."

Clémence paid the plumber, and he packed up to go.

"*Bonne journée!*" he said before he left.

"Have a nice day too," Clémence said.

"Can we at least split the cost?" Ben said.

"Nah."

"Okay, at least let me buy you a drink or something when you're at the poetry slam."

"Sure," Clémence said. "If that makes you feel better."

Ben dragged a crate of his dishes from the shower back to the small sink.

"I guess I'll clean up now."

Clémence noticed a wine glass with a lipstick stain on it. It was a shade of dark plum similar to the shade she'd seen in la gardienne's apartment.

"Who drank from your glass?" Clémence asked. "The one with the lipstick."

"Oh." Ben grinned. "I'm not having some sort of love affair if that's what you're thinking. Hope you're not jealous."

Clémence raised an eyebrow in amusement. "Oh please."

"Then why do you want to know?" Ben asked flirtatiously.

"Because I have a hunch," Clémence said. "Whoever she is, she was in la gardienne's apartment when she was killed."

"What?" Ben dropped the dopey smile. "Well, I mean, I guess it makes sense. It's the girl from next door, Lara. She was friends with la gardienne."

"Really? What does she do? Does she work for a family here?"

"Yes. She's a cleaner. She works for the family on the third floor sometimes and rents the room from them."

"Oh, the Dubois family?"

"Yes. Only part time because she works in other homes around the neighborhood too, and a couple of hair salons or something."

"Why is she friends with la gardienne?"

"Frankly, she and la gardienne like to gossip together about the tenants and what's happening in the building. Lara is not well liked by everyone else either. I think she has some sort of inferiority complex about being a maid. She's friendly toward me because I'm this poor writer and she thinks we're in the same social class." Ben chuckled. "The thing is, we've never really hung out, but last night, she knocked on my door and asked if I had any wine. I don't think she has too many friends, and she looked kind of harried. Maybe she was looking for company, and I did have some wine around, so we had a glass and chatted. She asked me a few questions about my day, and that was about it."

"That's weird. So she has never been in your room in the six months that you've lived here until last night?"

"Yes," Ben said. "Now that you've put it that way, I guess it is sort of strange. But it looked like she was upset about something and really needed a drink because she was out of alcohol. All the restaurants here are so expensive, and the stores are closed at night, so it made sense—I suppose—if she really wanted to drink. She kept chatting with me for a long time even though I could tell she was in her own thoughts sometimes."

"Unless she had just killed la gardienne and needed to see someone so she had an alibi," Clémence mused.

"What?" Ben frowned.

"I don't mean to scare you. I'm just looking at this from an inspector's perspective. Did she look odd in any way?"

"I don't think so," Ben said. "I mean, she wore a long-sleeved shirt that was scuffed up, but I think it's because she cleans in that shirt, so naturally she wasn't wearing her nicest clothes."

"What do you mean by scuffed up?"

"It was just an old gray shirt with some dirty stains here and there and some rips."

"Hmm."

"Wow, you really think she had something to do with the murder?"

"I don't know. I do think that I need to talk to her. She was in la gardienne's apartment last night, judging from the lipstick. What does she look like?"

"She's in her late twenties or early thirties—I can't tell. She has dark brown hair that she usually ties up in a knot on top of her head."

"And wears a plum-colored lipstick all the time?"

"Sometimes, yes."

"I wonder why she wanted to drink with you when she already had a drink with la gardienne."

Ben shrugged. "For the pleasure of my company?"

"What time does she usually come home?"

"Around seven or eight. I can usually hear her footsteps when she comes back. The walls are so thin, and I can pretty much tell who is coming and going just by their footsteps."

Clémence smiled wryly. "Great. Can you text me when she's home? I'll speak to her then."

"You're not going to just accuse her of murder, are you? She probably won't take too well to that. She does have a temper."

"A temper?"

"Yes. She's not hesitant to chew out a neighbor if they're playing their music too loud or something. I'm just lucky she doesn't mind me and I'm on her good side."

"Well, I'll be asking her about a cleaning job," Clémence said, "that has just become available at my place."

Chapter 7

Clémence went back to the patisserie to have some lunch. With all that had happened, she'd had no time to do her grocery shopping, so she had one of the chefs make her a salmon salad.

She invited Celine to join her to eat at the employee section after another hostess relieved Celine for her lunch break. She didn't speak to Celine about the murder. She didn't want to talk about it with anyone again until she spoke to Lara. Lunch was a time when murder shouldn't be on her mind. Instead, she chitchatted with Celine about girly things.

Celine had been talking about these new Burberry sandals she was drooling over, then she approached Clémence with a more delicate subject.

"You know Sebastien?" she started.

"Yup, what about him?"

"Well, I was wondering if you knew whether he had a girlfriend."

Clémence suppressed a smile. "Why so interested?"

Celine shrugged. "Just curiosity."

"Have you ever asked him?"

"No! I would never. It's none of my business."

"So why are you asking me?" Clémence teased.

Celine sighed. She ripped a piece off her baguette and popped it in her mouth. "Fine. I'm interested in him. But whenever we talk, it's always about desserts."

"That's Sebastien, all right."

"What's his deal? He's never flirty with me or anybody else. He only really talks to his sister." Celine sighed again, but this time with an airy smile. "He's so mysterious."

Clémence chuckled. Young love. She could see Sebastien's appeal. He was tall, with pale, perfect skin and sharp cheekbones. His big passion in life was his work: desserts. Plus, he was quiet, gentle, and thoughtful.

Clémence, however, preferred guys who were more outgoing and fun; but due to their spontaneous nature, they didn't think twice about breaking Clémence's heart.

"Why don't you ask Berenice?" asked Clémence.

Celine's eyes widened. "No way! She'll surely tell Sebastien that I like him. They're so close. But I can't stand it anymore. I need to know if Sebastien has a girlfriend. Otherwise, I can't seem to move on. I compare every guy with Sebastien, and I don't even know him that well."

"Workplace romances are a bit tricky," Clémence said. "Years ago, I dated one of the waiters—that was before you came to work here—and he expected special treatment after a while. Like he would come in late or ask for three or four days off at a time."

"Did you fire him?"

"My father did! He certainly didn't like the fact that we were together, which I suppose was part of the appeal. We continued dating for a couple of more weeks, but we soon realized that we had nothing in common outside of the patisserie. He had very little ambition in life. He got another job as a waiter in the fifteenth at a crappy brasserie, and I suspect that it will be his career." Clémence sighed at the memory. The waiter had been gorgeous but so wrong for her in every way. "But anyway, I can try to find out more about Sebastien from Berenice if you'd like. He is quiet, but he is actually quite observant."

"Thanks." Celine smiled in relief. "Seeing him is torture. I just want to break down those walls, you know? What is he thinking about all the time? What does he do outside of work? He drives me crazy. In a good way."

"Who knows, maybe once you get to know him, the appeal will be gone."

"I hope so," Celine said. "It's really throwing a wrench in my dating life. How am I supposed to enjoy myself out there when I'm in love with someone?"

"In love?"

"No, you know what I mean. Infatuated."

"Uh-huh." Clémence raised her eyebrows a few times to tease her, and Celine groaned.

"You're so embarrassing."

After Celine went back to her post at the front door with the other hostess, Clémence went into the kitchen to work on the desserts.

"How's the investigation going?" Berenice asked brightly.

Sebastien perked up with interest as well, his attention momentarily diverted from pistachio éclairs.

Clémence told them about Lara and the lipstick.

"You could be on to something," Berenice said. "So you're not going to tell the police about Lara?"

"Maybe they already know. But I figure if I talk to her under the pretense that I'm looking for a cleaner, maybe she'll be off her guard and tell me something she wouldn't tell the police."

"Now you're thinking like a sleuth," Berenice said. "Just be careful."

"My tenant Ben will be next door if anything happens," Clémence said.

"Ben, huh? Is he cute?"

"He is. He's the artsy type, which I like, I suppose, but I can't date him. He's a tenant. It'll be awkward."

"Is it also because he's poor?" Sebastien asked.

"No. It's just weird to be dating someone living in the same building. And I'll be seeing him all the time. He does laundry at my place."

"What's wrong with that?" asked Berenice.

"I need boundaries. Don't you guys?" Clémence figured this was the perfect opportunity to get Sebastien's dating status. "For example, dating at the workplace. Wouldn't you guys think it's odd? You'll have to see that person all the time if you break up."

Sebastien shrugged. "I suppose."

"I wouldn't mind," Berenice said. "If he's cute. Raoul's pretty cute. I'd date him if he asked me."

"What about you, Seb? Who'd you date here?"

Sebastien shrugged again and turned his attention back to his éclairs.

Berenice rolled her eyes. "He's hopeless with women. Last night, we were in a pub, and these two English girls kept flirting with him, and he did nothing. He didn't even buy them a drink and only gave one-word answers."

"I didn't like them," Sebastien said matter-of-factly. "They were too loud for my taste, and they kept asking me questions."

"What exactly *is* your taste?" Clémence said.

"She has to be soft, light, and sweet."

"So your next girlfriend is going to be a meringue?" Clémence laughed.

Berenice joined her. Even Sebastien couldn't suppress a smile.

"Oh, forget him," Berenice said, going back to work on her tray of chocolate éclairs. "He's way too picky for a guy. It's because he was heartbroken once. Badly."

Sebastien cleared his throat and shifted uncomfortably. "Can we talk about something else? The murder case, perhaps? Or these new macarons that Clémence wants to make?"

"I prefer to work on the macarons," Clémence said. "Let's work on the lychee-flavored recipe. I just ordered a fresh case of lychees, and we can start making them soon. There's also green tea matcha powder that's being shipped from Japan, courtesy of my mother. We should get it tomorrow. Speaking of my mother, I should really call her to ask her about the other tenants in my building.

But shoot, I have to go to the police station now to give my statement. Plus, I still have to shop for groceries!"

Clémence grabbed her coat.

"Busy girl." Berenice tsk-tsked after her.

Chapter 8

Clémence went to 36 Quai des Orfèvres, the headquarters of the Paris criminal police, at Île de la Cité in the first arrondissement. She walked up to the first floor and told the guy at the front desk what she was there for. He was perfectly unhelpful. He told her in a snappy, impatient tone to sit in the waiting area.

Clémence did what she was told—at first. Forty minutes passed, and the guy at the front had disappeared for the last fifteen. Did Cyril even know she was there?

She decided to take a walk down the hall. The doors of the offices were marked with the names and positions, and she spotted Inspector Cyril St. Clair's office. Before she knocked, she couldn't help overhearing snippets of conversation.

"*Deux semaines?* It's going to take two weeks to get the DNA hair sample results back? What are these guys doing? *Oh là là.*" It was Cyril's whiny voice.

"They're backlogged, sir. But they did find out that the button belongs to a man's Burberry trench coat."

"Great," Cyril muttered. "Now we're just going to have to find all the men who wear Burberry trench coats and find out who's missing a button—if they haven't gotten a new one sewn on already."

Cyril sighed in exasperation. Clémence knew the investigation wasn't going well, and she couldn't help but feel a bit smug; Cyril had been so nasty and arrogant to her.

"They are making progress with the handwriting sample," his colleague said.

"I want results, not progress. Now, who would be blackmailing her—"

Suddenly they grew silent. They must've noticed her shadow through the door's window. Clémence backed away. She should learn how to eavesdrop properly.

"Who's there?" Cyril barked.

Clémence opened the door. Cyril's face fell at the sight of her. "Oh. You."

"I'm here to give my statement to the police," Clémence said. "I waited for a long time."

"Fine." Cyril sighed again.

He waved his colleague to leave and gestured for Clémence to sit down.

"I take it that the investigation is going well?" Clémence smiled at him brightly, making Cyril glower even more because he knew that she had heard.

"Very well," Cyril said. "We have a hair sample and someone's cup with a lipstick stain, and we'll know who was in that room with her that evening as soon as we get the DNA results back. If you're lucky, you'll be off the hook."

Clémence thought that chances were high that the hair belonged to Lara, but she didn't want to tell Cyril yet—not until she talked to her—so he wouldn't ruin her investigation with his accusations and incompetence.

Her investigation. Was she really trying to solve a murder? She did feel partly responsible. La gardienne had been eating her macarons when she was killed, and it did happen in her building.

She couldn't understand why Cyril didn't just inquire of the tenants of the building whether anyone had seen someone wearing a lipstick shade of that color. They would probably find Lara in no time. But men were clueless about things like makeup and which colors were popular and which ones were not.

There was also the paper on la gardienne's table. Had she been writing a letter? Or perhaps one of the instructional signs she had around the building? There were already signs up warning residents to tie up garbage bags so as not to attract flies, to flush the public toilets better, and to not put plastic bags in the recycling bins.

And what was this about blackmail? Somebody was blackmailing la gardienne?

She wanted to ask him about the note and the blackmail, but she thought better of it. He would probably not tell her anything and would suspect her for knowing too much.

After she'd given her statement of everything Cyril had already known, she went home and tried her mother on the phone.

"How are you, *chérie*?" her mother asked.

"It hasn't exactly been the smoothest homecoming."

Clémence told her all about the murder and how the inspector had had the nerve to accuse her.

"*Mon dieu!* She's worked there forever. A murder in our own building?"

Clémence told her the inspector was useless. It was up to her to help solve the case.

"*Fait attention*," her mother warned. "Be careful. We're talking about a murderer here."

"I know, *maman*; I just want to help. I mean, the inspector is probably going around questioning people in his foul-tempered way. If I do the questioning, I might actually get some answers. Now, would you know who would be an enemy of la gardienne's?"

"Everyone's had trouble with her," she said. "Just everyone. She complains when we put garbage in the wrong containers, if we get in too late and wake her up with our footsteps, if too many of our guests are coming and going if we have a party—everything. For the past couple of months, she's been threatening to quit because she was so fed up with everyone."

"But I suppose someone's fed up with her too. But who?"

"I don't know the neighbors in the other building, but in our building, I've seen her arguing with the dentist once. I was just coming out of the elevator, and the dentist was red faced when he walked back up to his office on the first floor."

"Any idea what that was about?"

"No. I didn't hear what they were saying, but la gardienne looked really self-satisfied, as if she'd won whatever conversation or argument they had." She thought a bit more. "Then there was the incident with the Dubois family. The kids are troublemakers, and they don't like la gardienne. They like to throw things down at her when they see her down in the courtyard, but the parents would cover up for them and tell her that it wasn't them. The parents really coddle their kids in a way that I don't approve of."

Clémence agreed. She could imagine Arthur being a total mama's boy, judging from how spoiled he was.

"What are you saying?" Clémence asked. "You think the Duboises could be suspects?"

"Suspects? No, I don't believe they are murderers. I don't want to believe that any of them are! They're my neighbors. I've known them for years!"

"What do you know about the dentist, then?"

"Phillipe? He seems friendly enough, but since I go to another dentist, I don't interact with him often. He just works during office hours and lives in Boulogne-Billancourt, I think, so I don't run into him as often as the rest. I don't really know much about him."

"What about Lara, the cleaner? She's friends with la gardienne, right?"

"Oh, she's rude. Whenever I say '*bonjour*' to her, she never says it back!"

"That's all you have against her?" Clémence laughed.

"Well, it's common courtesy. I don't know much else about her except that she works for the Dubois family. I can't even get a hello out of her, so how would I?"

Clémence supposed she was really going to have to question Lara herself.

Chapter 9

When Ben texted her that he'd heard Lara come home, Clémence went up the servant staircase through the kitchen. Lara lived in Room 14. Clémence knocked and plastered a smile on her face.

Lara opened the door roughly, in the same abrupt manner as la gardienne. It was as if they were so annoyed at being disturbed that they wanted to scare the person away with their sudden appearance at the door.

The woman poked her head out without a smile. Her plum lipstick was faded on her lips, and her long brown hair was knotted in a messy bun at the top of her head. Her eyes were dark and sharp like a hawk's. She was barefoot and was clutching a glass of wine. At the sight of Clémence, her eyes narrowed suspiciously.

"*Bonsoir.*" Clémence kept the smile on her face. "Are you Lara?"

"*Oui.*"

"I'm Clémence Damour from the fifth floor, and I was wondering if I could talk to you for a minute?"

Lara gave her a nasty once-over. She must've learned that from la gardienne as well. They really did spend a lot of time together.

"Sure. What is it?"

"Well, I heard that you're a cleaner, and I'm looking for someone to clean occasionally."

"I thought you already had one," she said roughly.

"Yes, but she only comes once a week. I like to have parties sometimes, and I was wondering if you'd be interested in small jobs here and there when my regular cleaner is not available."

Lara put a cigarette in her mouth and lit up. She inhaled and blew the smoke out from one side of her lips, but the smell still aggravated Clémence. Cigarette smoke was Clémence's pet peeve, and it was one of the major things that she hadn't missed about Paris when she had been away.

"How much does it pay?" Lara asked.

Clémence gave her a ballpark figure, and Lara's eyes lit up.

"Fine," she said. "You have my number?"

"No, I'll take it."

Lara wrote it down on a Post-it note and gave it to her.

"Oh, and I heard that you were friends with la gardienne. I'm sorry for your tragic loss."

Lara's face dropped at the mention of her. Was it out of guilt or sadness?

"Yes. Thank you. We were friends." Her voice was lifeless.

"Did you talk to her at all before she died?"

Lara took her time sucking on her cigarette. Her lips tensed up, and Clémence could imagine her forty years later with wrinkles all around her lips and her skin leathery like certain older French women.

"We did have a drink," Lara said. "In the early evening."

Lara shook her head as if she wanted to shake the memory away.

"Is that something you do often?" Clémence asked as casually as possible.

"Every once in a while, I suppose. She's the closest thing to family here."

"She never had her own children?"

"No. Her husband left her for another woman thirty years ago."

"I see. Who do you think could've done this to her?"

Lara's eyes turned red. Tears formed. Then again, it could've been the cigarette smoke. Clémence's eyes were tearing up as well. She'd always been sensitive to smoke in close quarters, and her father had to give up smoking after she was born in order to be around her.

"I don't know," Lara said. "There's a lot of people in this building, and none of them had a good relationship with her. She was so fed up with everything that she was talking about saving up some money and leaving."

"Where would she have gone?" Clémence asked.

"No idea. But she seemed very happy about the prospect of leaving. Said she almost had enough money saved up."

"Have you noticed if she'd been in any disagreements with anybody in the building recently?"

Lara sighed.

"Well, in general, people were not closing their trash bags properly before tossing them down the chutes. They were attracting flies, so she hated everybody for being so inconsiderate. People also mixed up garbage in the recycling bins, so that had been driving her crazier than usual." Lara thought about it some more. "Before I came yesterday, I did see the dentist coming out of her apartment. He had some letters in his hand, so maybe she'd given him his mail, but it was strange because she didn't really like people going into her apartment. Once, an old man fell on the street and was bleeding, and instead of letting him rest in her apartment as he waited for the ambulance, she brought a chair out for him."

Clémence nodded. It was strange to hear that the dentist had gone into her apartment. La gardienne usually delivered the mail to each door.

"Well, anyway, I don't know who would do it," Lara said. "Too many people hate her."

Even you? Clémence silently wondered.

"Well, thanks." Clémence shook the Post-it note in her hand. "I'll give you a call if I ever need anyone."

"Great," Lara said with no enthusiasm.

A slam of the door, and she was out of sight.

Clémence didn't know what to make of Lara. She certainly tried to show as little emotion as possible, but Clémence had caught a glimpse of some emotion in her eyes. Lara definitely had feelings. Clémence just couldn't tell whether she was guilty and trying to hide it or was sad for the loss of her only friend and trying not to look vulnerable.

She was still on her suspect list. There was something that Lara was hiding, but she didn't know what. But there was also this dentist. Both her mother and Lara had mentioned his being at odds with la gardienne, and that didn't sound good.

Clémence had never met the dentist and wouldn't recognize him if she happened to pass him. She didn't know a lot of people in the building.

What if she never found the killer? Would the killer just live amongst them?

Chapter 10

Clémence poured fresh raspberries into the bowl.

In the Damour kitchen, she, Sebastien, and Berenice were onto their newest flavor—lychee with raspberry buttercream filling. The lychee macaron shells were baking in the oven, and they were working on the cream filling.

The kitchen was always full of sweet aromas. It was a scent that Clémence had grown up with. She felt most comfortable in a kitchen, and baking was a way to get creative. It was a good way to start the day because she had been tossing and turning in bed the previous night, thinking about the case and what she should ask the dentist.

She had managed to make a last-minute appointment with the dentist for a checkup later that day, thanks to a cancellation. She already had a dentist in the fifth arrondissement whom she quite liked, but it wouldn't be so bad to have a dentist in the same building. Unless, of course, he was a cold-blooded killer.

She never managed to buy her groceries, and she'd given up and just ordered them online. It was what her mother usually did anyway. The local supermarket would deliver them to her the next day. Clémence was a busy working woman now, even if working was really experimenting with baked goods in the "lab."

So far, their green-tea macarons hadn't been quite right. Berenice thought they were okay, but she didn't have the extremely high standards that both Sebastien and Clémence took upon themselves. They were the highest of dessert snobs.

"It has to be perfect," Clémence said.

"Don't worry," Sebastien reassured her. "It will be."

"Oh, you guys are nerds," Berenice said.

Clémence and Sebastien's perfectionist tendencies drove her crazy, so she wanted no part in their projects. She was in her corner, making chocolate truffles. "How's the case going, anyway?"

Clémence sighed. "It's frustrating. No wonder that lame inspector throws hissy fits. It's confusing because there are so many potential suspects. I don't even know most of the tenants who live in my building. But I am going to speak to this dentist later today, and maybe he'll have some answers."

"Dentist?" Berenice asked.

Clémence told her what Lara had said.

"Be careful," Sebastien said. "What if he drugs you?"

Clémence laughed at his melodramatic concern. "It's just a checkup. Besides, he has staff and other patients in his office. I doubt he can harm me. You know how thin the walls are."

"If the walls are so thin, why didn't anyone hear la gardienne getting killed?"

"The dentist is on the first floor, and a pediatrician is on the second floor. There's also a dermatologist's office across from la gardienne's apartment, which divides our two buildings from the other two buildings around the courtyard. All these offices would be empty at night. La gardienne's room is closer to the front door than the courtyard, so their voices would've been hard to hear."

"But her apartment is by the front door, right?" Sebastien said. "Wouldn't there be people coming and going, even if it's late?"

"I suppose there could be," Clémence said. "But most of the people in my building are older. I doubt they'd be partying or staying out too late. Although, there are some teenagers and people my age. The inspector has probably interrogated most of the people in the building. I saw him snooping around this morning. He was going up the stairs when I descended by elevator, so he didn't see me. I wonder if he has found out anything new."

"You can ask him," Berenice said.

"I just might," Clémence said. "If he does find anything, I'm sure that he'd be eager to brag about it."

Berenice rolled her eyes. "Typical."

"Oh, by the way, my tenant Ben invited me to his poetry slam tonight. Do you guys want to go?"

"Is it in English?" Berenice asked.

"It is."

"Oh, my English is not very good. I'm not sure."

"Come on, you can learn. I'm sure there will be lots of young, artsy guys, the kinds you love."

"You mean hipsters," Sebastien said. "Or *Bobos*."

"Bobo" was short for Bohemian Bourgeois, a French version of the "richster"—rich hipsters, the young bourgeoisie who preferred to live in "real" neighborhoods.

"But you're a Bobo," Berenice said.

"No, I'm not," Sebastien said. "I'm just a normal French guy."

Clémence snorted. "What does that even mean?"

"I don't pretend to be poor when I'm rich, and I don't pretend to be rich when I'm poor. I'm just a guy content with my status in life."

"*N'importe quoi*," Berenice said. "Whatever. So are you coming tonight, or what?"

"To hear a bunch of pretentious poetry in some dingy basement of a crappy pub? No thank you."

"How do you know it's in *une cave*?" Clémence asked.

"Isn't it?"

"Well, yes. But—"

A small, self-satisfied smile appeared on his lips.

"Know-it-all," Clémence muttered. Sometimes Sebastien was too smart for his own good. "My friend Rose is coming; so is Celine. Are you sure you don't want to go, Sebastien? Lots of lovely la-a-adies."

Sebastien shook his head. "Can't. I'm busy."

He didn't care to elaborate on what he was busy with.

"Why, what are you up to?" Clémence asked casually.

"Are you investigating my personal life?" Sebastien asked, a small smile curling on his lips.

"I'm just curious. God, you're so mysterious."

"Good," he said. "Girls love mysteries."

"I don't even know what he gets up to," Berenice said. "I think he's dating someone."

The girls looked at Sebastien. He turned a shade pinker.

"Don't you girls have a murder to investigate? I'm too discreet to talk about my love life."

Berenice sighed. "I'm your sister. I always tell you about the guys I date."

"Thanks for sharing, but I never ask to begin with."

Clémence shook her head. Too clever and too mysterious. No wonder Celine was mad about him. Even she was curious what he was up to in his spare time. She knew that Sebastien lived alone in the fifth arrondissement, the Latin Quarter. Berenice still lived in her parents' big apartment in the second.

When she went out to chat with Celine on her way out, she had to give her the bad news.

"He's not coming, sweetie," Clémence said. "Says he's busy but won't tell me why."

"I'm going to kill him," she fumed. "But forget him. We'll find some cute guys tonight."

"For sure," Clémence said.

But she wasn't so sure. Love wasn't a priority right now. To her, love had always been messy. She was too easily attached and would rather be alone than have her heart broken again so soon. For now, she would just enjoy Paris with her friends, new and old.

Chapter 11

After grabbing a tuna baguette sandwich to go from Damour, Clémence went home to feed and play with Miffy a bit.

"Did you miss me, girl?"

Miffy panted, stretching her lips in a way that looked like a smile. She ran to her play den and brought back a pink toy bone for Clémence as an offering. Clémence played with Miffy a little more and filled her bowl with dog food before she turned her attention to her sandwich.

Clémence would've felt guilty for leaving Miffy home alone, but her parents had reassured her that Miffy was a very independent dog who could spend hours entertaining herself. Clémence could bring her along to the patisserie kitchen sometimes, but her dad had told her that Miffy was content either way.

All Clémence needed to do was spend a good half hour playing with Miffy if she planned to be out of the house for less than three hours at a time. All the furniture remained pristine; Miffy would've been chewing furniture if she was upset or lonely, so Clémence's guilt eased. Miffy must've been an introverted dog who needed time alone to recharge. Later that afternoon, Clémence would walk her, so Miffy would get some social interaction in her day as well.

After lunch, she prepared for her dentist appointment. Naturally, she brushed her teeth after eating, as dentists could be quite judgmental sometimes. Then she searched the Internet for more information on the dentist, Phillipe Rousseau. He had a website, where he was featured on the home page with his arms crossed and smiling, showing off his perfect white teeth. He had salt-and-pepper hair and a friendly smile. He sounded like an upstanding guy according to the testimonials on his site from his clients, but it wasn't as if he would include anything other than glowing reviews.

That was the only info on Phillipe Rousseau that she could find. The other links that came up in the search were not for dentists. All she knew at this point was that he was a handsome older man with a solid reputation. Although her parents had gone to the same dentist for years due to habit, they did seem to think he was nice as a neighbor. Her mother had mentioned exchanging pleasantries with him once or twice.

What could he have been so worked up about regarding la gardienne? And what had he been doing in her apartment the night she was killed?

She went downstairs and checked in with the receptionist at the dental office. It was interesting because the office was laid out like her apartment, but most of the rooms contained a dentist chair. Clémence waited, browsing through *Paris Match* magazine. She read about the latest love affair of the country's president. The scandal had read like a soap opera, and Clémence had to laugh at the melodrama of it all. What were these women thinking? She would somewhat understand if he was handsome, like the dentist, but their president was not attractive in the least.

The man of the hour appeared. His hair was whiter than in his website photos, but his smile matched. His teeth were so unnaturally white that she was sure they would've glowed if the lights were turned off. Clémence wondered if she should be bleaching her teeth too.

"Ah, Mademoiselle Damour," he said. "I've heard a lot about you from your mother."

"My mother certainly likes to chat," Clémence laughed.

He showed her into the room, and she sat down in the dentist chair.

"I heard you've been traveling around for two years."

"Yes, but I assure you, I still managed to get my teeth cleaned every six months."

Phillipe chuckled. "What was the favorite place that you've visited?"

"Oh gosh, I can't pick. It depends. I supposed I quite liked Croatia's beaches. And Thailand was pretty insane."

"Are you glad to be back in Paris?"

Phillipe was asking all the questions, but Clémence answered politely, figuring it might make it easier for her to ask him questions later on.

"Oh yes. I missed the pastries."

"Be careful of cavities."

"I'm surprised we don't have more cavities than we do in our family," Clémence said. "But we're very consistent with oral care. Plus, I'm glad that we have a dentist in the building. It's so convenient."

"Yes, for if you ever have a dental emergency." Phillipe pushed a button, and the chair went down. He put on his face mask. "Let's take a look here."

After much probing, Phillipe told her that her teeth were pristine.

"If only all my clients were like you." He lowered his voice. "Some of them you wouldn't believe. Even in this neighborhood."

Clémence suppressed a smile. It was her cue to begin her line of questioning.

"Yes, well, we're not like the Americans, who put braces on their kids almost as soon as they're born."

Phillipe chuckled again. "But I don't disagree with their methods."

Clémence could see why he was such a hit with his clients. He was the nicest French dentist she'd ever met. The other ones had only reprimanded her for not brushing enough. It was easy to get swept up in Phillipe's charm and compliments.

"Speaking of this neighborhood," Clémence started. "It's a shame about la gardienne, huh?"

"Yes," Phillipe said without a beat. "Awful."

"I mean, she's not very well liked, but I can't believe someone would do this, and in our building too."

"I don't believe it either."

"Did you know her well?"

"Not well," he said. "She often wanted to chat at inconvenient times, like when I was coming to work. I think she had a little crush on me, really."

"A crush on you?" Clémence said.

"Well, don't tell my wife, or she'd get jealous, but la gardienne was always trying to make excuses to see me, and she made me go inside her apartment a couple of times when I was going home from work. She claimed that she had toothaches. I'd quickly check her teeth, but both times they were fine. I was pretty sure that she was faking it to get attention."

"Wow, that sounds..."

"Desperate, I know. But she's a lonely woman with nothing to do all day but to listen in on other people's conversations and get into the residents' business. She was always trying to tell me what she knew, as if I'd be interested in her gossip."

"What *did* she know?" Clémence asked.

"Funny, the inspector asked me the same thing this morning. But I suppose this is common gossip in the building anyhow. Apparently, the cleaner who lives on the roof—do you know her? I think her name is Lara."

"I might have seen her around," Clémence said vaguely.

"Well, I think that she's having a love affair with Arthur Dubois, from the third floor."

"Oh?"

"Yes, and Madame Dubois is not very pleased with it."

"Wow, really?"

Clémence could see why Madame Dubois wouldn't be very pleased. She wanted her son to date only upper-class girls, but it had always seemed that Arthur had a thing for forbidden fruit.

Chapter 12

It all made sense... or did it? Lara and Arthur were in love, and la gardienne was going to expose them, so Lara whacked her. Or Arthur whacked her. Was Arthur even the type to fall in love? Something more must've been at stake here, but what? Money?

Clémence considered asking Lara but figured she would have to question Arthur anyway, even if he was the embodiment of the type of man she detested. It wouldn't be hard. He usually walked the family dog at night, before dinner. She could walk Miffy later than usual and casually join him.

After she left the dentist office, she pressed the elevator button to go back up to the fifth floor. The door opened to reveal Inspector Cyril St. Clair inside the elevator.

Clémence inwardly groaned. Cyril didn't look too enthused to see her either and gave a grudging "*bonjour.*" Even at his rudest, a proper Frenchman couldn't not say hello.

"Am I still a suspect?" Clémence asked. She was squeezed tight next to the inspector in the tiny elevator, even though he was tall and thin.

"You're lucky," he said. "We didn't find any evidence against you. But I still have my eye on you."

"Did you find *anyone's* fingerprints or anything?"

"That is none of your business."

The elevator stopped on the third floor.

"Oh, so is a Dubois a suspect?" Clémence asked.

"Stay out of it," Cyril groaned.

He stepped out, pulling on his trench coat so it wouldn't get stuck between the closing elevator doors. In the spring, many men wore these light beige-colored jackets. It was either that or black jackets. Many Frenchmen dressed in the same classic style. Clémence recalled the wooden button. She wondered if Arthur had a jacket like that. She usually saw him in his lame cashmere sweaters in a variety of colors, so she didn't know. Perhaps she could slip that question into the conversation as well.

Clémence had been watching the street from her balcony for the past hour and a half. Finally, she saw him: Arthur Dubois walking his Jack Russell terrier in his calm, leisurely way.

"Come on!" she exclaimed to Miffy. It was showtime.

The elevator took too long to come, so they scurried down the carpeted stairs and rushed out onto the street. Arthur was nowhere in sight, so he must've turned a corner. She and Miffy ran. Miffy looked happy; her tongue was out, and at times she looked at Clémence sideways with what looked like a smile.

Finally, they spotted him waiting for the traffic to stop so he could cross the street around Trocadéro's roundabout.

They followed him as he walked past the Cité de l'Architecture and all the tourists taking photos. Arthur didn't stop to admire the Eiffel Tower like everyone else. The sun was setting, and people were very appreciative of the view. There was even a professional photo shoot taking place, with an Amazonian brunette standing high in designer heels and a flowing lavender dress. A photographer was snapping away while his assistant was bouncing light off a reflector at the model's face.

Clémence took in the aroma of the waffle-and-crêpe stand. She threw a few admiring glances at La Tour but tried to keep focused on Arthur. He was going down the steps to the park. There was a long fountain downstairs, and Arthur walked along one side. He was heading for the Champs de Mars, Clémence was sure.

After he crossed the Seine River, they were there. The Eiffel Tower, now a dusty rose color, loomed above them in her greatness. Clémence sighed. When it came to La Tour, she never ceased to be a tourist. Arthur didn't seem fazed at all. Then again, he had probably been living in the sixteenth all his life and was too used to the view.

People picnicked on the grass, drinking wine and eating baguettes with cheese. Clémence had shared some fun memories in the past with her friends on the Champs de Mars, but where there were tourists in Paris, there were pickpockets. Once, her cell phone had almost been taken from her picnic blanket when she wasn't careful.

Arthur was still leisurely strolling up ahead. She closed in until they were fifteen feet apart. Clémence's plan was to casually bump into him, but Miffy was too eager. At the sight of Arthur's dog, she barked and pulled at her leash. Arthur's Jack Russell turned back and recognized her too. Arthur turned around and noticed Clémence.

The dogs reunited like old friends, licking each other's faces and wagging their tails in happiness.

"Looks like they missed each other," Clémence laughed.

A smile even spread on Arthur's face. She'd never even seen anything close to a smile on him before. He was very smartly dressed tonight—none of his usual sweaters. Instead, he wore a light-blue dress shirt and an olive-colored hunting jacket with dark-blue jeans. His chestnut hair was neatly combed as always, and his dark eyes were smoldering in the twilight.

He bent down to stroke Miffy.

"*Coucou*," he whispered to her. "Hey, girl."

Miffy licked his hand, and it seemed like she wanted to jump into his arms. Clémence was surprised to discover that Arthur had a soft side. He really was a dog lover.

"It looks like she missed you too," Clémence remarked.

Arthur looked up at her. His brown eyes were the exact shade of his hair. His lips were full, and his skin was translucent and flawless. She could see why girls would fall for him. Clémence, however, was not easily swayed by good looks. Arthur did have a big personality defect, not to mention that he was on the top of her suspect list for murdering la gardienne.

"So you're walking your dog at Champs de Mars now?" he asked briskly. It sounded more like an accusation than small talk.

"Yes. I like this park. Where else would I walk Miffy?"

"It's a bit far from the house, don't you think? Your father used to walk around the block."

"Well, I prefer parks," Clémence said defensively. "And this is where Miffy would meet other dogs, and I want her to be social."

Arthur didn't say much more. He began walking when the dogs did; they were happily strolling side by side. Clémence followed. If Arthur hadn't been a suspect, she would've turned the other way. Something about him repelled her. It was the same way Cyril repelled her—the arrogance, the entitlement, the haughty attitude.

"A shame about the murder, isn't it?" Clémence offered.

"The murder? Oh, la gardienne. Yeah. Weird stuff."

His face was inscrutable.

"Did you know her well at all?" she pressed.

"Not really. I don't think many people did."

"Well, what about Lara?"

"Our cleaner? Yes, I have seen them talking. I think they're friends."

Clémence wasn't getting much out of him, and she had to up her game.

"Lara's quite pretty, isn't she?"

"I suppose." His jaw seemed to clench. "What about it?"

"Oh, nothing. I think she mentioned once that she found you handsome."

Arthur gave a snort. "You think I would go out with her? She's our cleaner."

He sounded too offended—or defensive?—and Clémence suspected that she had hit a nerve.

"What about it? She's still beautiful."

"Her French grammar is awful," he said. "Not to mention that she can't hold a decent conversation at all."

That's funny, Clémence thought. *Talking to you is like pulling teeth.*

Clémence had enough of his arrogance. She cut to the chase. "So you're not dating?"

Arthur gave her a funny look. "Are you kidding me? Why would you think that we're dating?"

Clémence averted her eyes from his burning stare.

"I thought I heard a rumor." She shrugged.

"From whom?"

"Just someone in the building."

"There's not even an ounce of truth to that," Arthur said. His face was beet red. "I can't believe that you'd think that."

"Well, I don't know you that well," Clémence said.

"I'm not involved with Lara." Arthur rubbed his face in agitation. His pale skin became red and irritated. "My father is."

"Excuse me?"

"My father. He's having an affair with Lara. I didn't think anybody else knew, but everybody seems to know everybody else's business in that building."

Clémence wanted to smack herself. "Is your father's name Arthur as well?"

"Yes. I wish I wasn't named after the bastard. He cheats on my mother right under our noses and thinks we're too dumb to notice."

Of course. It was Arthur Dubois Sr. How could she have been so clueless?

"How many of your siblings know about the affair?"

"Not the younger ones, but Theo does, and so does Matilde."

"What about your mother?"

Arthur laughed bitterly. "She probably doesn't. She's too busy shopping and lunching to notice."

"And if she does find out?"

"I don't know. The girl will be cast out, of course, but I reckon my mother will still stay with my father."

"But why?"

"Why?" He shook his head. "My mother has stayed with him for various reasons other than for the pleasure of his company."

"I didn't know. I'm sorry–"

"That's okay," he cut in abruptly. "My family is messed up, all right? I can't wait to move out."

"What's stopping you?"

"My siblings. And I need to finish my PhD." She had assumed that he was doing very little with his life.

"I didn't know you were doing a PhD."

"You don't want to know about it," Arthur said. "It's too boring. I don't even want to talk about it."

They walked around the park in silence. The silence made Clémence uncomfortable. She wanted to leave Arthur alone out of respect. Sure, she felt bad that his family was screwed up, but there was nothing she could do or say.

When they turned to walk back toward the tower, Arthur spoke.

"Now, tell me about the desserts you're making at Damour."

Chapter 13

Clémence was surprised to find herself enjoying a walk with someone whom she had suspected of being a murderer only an hour ago. Arthur was actually sweet and incredibly bright despite his sardonic and snide humor, found in many Parisian men. He wasn't the spoiled playboy who mooched off his parents' wealth. Well, he was partly that, but he was more vulnerable than he let on. She supposed that was how men worked. How people worked. The more vulnerable they were, the tougher they acted.

Clémence found herself suppressing the urge to give Arthur a hug by the time they reached the tower again. Maybe it was the last pink glimpse of the sun. Maybe it was the tinkling chatter of the picnickers. Maybe it was La Tour, the symbol of romance around the world standing over them. She felt a bit light-headed—intoxicated—and overwhelmed by everything.

She looked at her watch.

"I have to go," she said. "I'm late."

They were walking back home together, but Clémence tugged Miffy away from Arthur's Jack Russell. She didn't know whether to give Arthur bisous goodbye. Were they friends now after their intimate conversation? She didn't know, but she hadn't been lying when she said that she was late. A simple American wave sufficed, and Arthur waved back, a hand up like a white flag, his face melancholy in the evening darkness.

Berenice, Celine, and Rose were waiting for her at Métro Oberkampf in the eleventh arrondissement. Clémence dropped Miffy off at home and gave her a treat. She quickly changed into something more chic—houndstooth cigarette pants, a black V-neck tee, a black leather jacket, and blue velvet ballet flats—and scurried out again.

When she was on a train, she texted her friends to say that she was running about ten minutes late. She would meet them at the bar if they could just save her a seat. Then she calmed down a bit. A train seat became available, and she sat down and thought about the events of the day.

So Monsieur Dubois was having an affair with Lara. La gardienne knew about the affair and told the dentist, who told her. So what had la gardienne been doing with that information that made Lara so upset the night the old woman was murdered?

Perhaps la gardienne had threatened to expose them. Paris was one of the most expensive cities in the world. Lara probably lived in her little apartment on the cheap, and if she was cast out, she would have a hard time finding affordable housing in Paris.

Or what about Dubois? He might risk losing his wife, his family, and his money from a divorce.

La gardienne had been saving up some money to escape, hadn't she? So she could've blackmailed Dubois for her nest egg.

And the wooden button was from a man's jacket. It seemed likely that Dubois Sr. was the type to wear a Burberry jacket. Clémence had never met the guy, however.

When she changed Métro lines, she called her mother's cell phone.

"Hello, dear. We're having dim sum in Hong Kong!"

Her mother sounded like she was having the time of her life.

"It's on the twentieth floor of a building here on Hong Kong Island, and we can see the mountains and the city. It's incredibly romantic."

Her father cut in.

"Clémence? Is that you, *chérie*?"

"Hi, Dad. I've missed you."

"Wish you were here too. The pork buns we're eating are absolutely delectable. Although it was hell deciphering the menu. I don't read Chinese! Luckily, the waiter was able to translate."

Clémence was happy to hear updates about her parents' travels. The Damour patisserie and tea salon in Hong Kong would open in two weeks, and they were prepping for their grand opening. On their days off, they were exploring the exciting city. Hong Kong was formerly a British colony, so the city was a mix of East and West.

"The shopping here is amazing," her mother piped up. "I found a nice cashmere shawl for you. It's pink, your favorite color."

"Merci, I'm sure I'll love it. By the way, I was just wondering, have you ever seen Monsieur Dubois from the third floor wearing a Burberry jacket?"

"What kind of Burberry jacket? The classic trench?"

"Sure," Clémence said. "Any Burberry jacket."

"Well, I suppose so. Why?"

"Nothing. I just found this button and thought it might belong to him."

"Yes," her mother said. "I'm sure he has at least one jacket from Burberry. He's very fashionable."

Chapter 14

The basement of the bar was boiling hot. The sweaty audience sat on short benches. They were squeezed around a little stage with a single bright spotlight shining down on it. Glasses of wine and pints of beer were flowing freely to distract the people from the heat.

Clémence bought a glass of rosé and went down to *la cave*. The event was running late, and people were still chatting. She found her girlfriends sitting on a bench near the front, and she went over to greet them.

"Hey, stranger." A pretty blonde greeted her with *bisous*.

Rose had been friends with Clémence since they were thirteen. Rose had even joined her in Australia for a week a month ago. She was now working at a PR firm and living in the 6th with her boyfriend.

"Where is Pierre, anyway?"

"He's too tired to come out," Rose said.

"Have you met Ben yet?" Clémence asked her friends.

"No," Berenice said. "We don't know what he looks like."

Clémence looked around and found him in the back corner chatting with a guy wearing a fedora and a tank top.

"Ben!" she called and waved.

He came over with his friend, and Clémence made the introductions.

"This is my friend Sam," Ben said. "He's from Manchester."

Sam had a dirty-blond shag and a dimpled grin. He was a little on the short side, but he seemed to possess plenty of charm. The boys chatted with the girls for a few minutes before the room darkened and the emcee announced that the night of poetry and debauchery was about to begin.

The first couple of acts were forgettable. Clémence realized that she didn't exactly like spoken poetry. She preferred to read poems and devour each word to reflect on its meaning. Poetry read out loud was more like a performance that she didn't quite understand.

One girl read a poem complaining about being seen and treated as a sexual object. Clémence couldn't help but interpret her poem as a long brag about how beautiful she was. Then another performer sang and played guitar. He was French and sang in English with a thick French accent, and she had no idea what he was singing about at all.

After about eight acts, Clémence was thinking that the whole thing was kind of lame. Then Ben stepped on the stage.

He looked strong underneath the spotlight. Dressed in his signature black clothes with his nearly black hair and paper-white skin, he looked like a haunted figure in one of those Gothic Victorian novels, like Mr. Rochester in *Jane Eyre*.

His voice had a lovely cadence when he read, and Clémence quickly got absorbed in his poem, "The Black Cat." It was about a lonely cat walking along Parisian rooftops spying on neighbors through their windows: families arguing, children playing, happy singles, lonely souls. The black cat finally goes into the apartment of an old bachelor and curls up at his feet.

What Clémence liked about his reading was that he was telling a story, and it completely pulled her in. She felt a little like the black cat, trying to spy on her neighbors. It got her thinking about the case again. She wondered if the inspector had found anything yet.

Sam read after him. He read faster, almost rapping, talking about the finer points of living in Manchester and the homeless people he often encountered.

They were both talented. The girls congratulated and complimented them when the set was over. The boys seemed to grow taller with each admiring glance and kind word from the beautiful French girls. Upstairs near the bar, they all ended up drinking around a table.

"*Vive la Paris!*" Ben stood up on his chair with his wine glass up, saluting everyone at the bar. Some patrons cheered back. The mood in the bar was jolly, and it reminded Clémence of the great night she'd had in Mexico with her friends a year ago. She loved the nights when everyone got together and had fun. It made her feel less lonely, less like the black cat.

She was glad to see Celine flirting with Sam. Maybe she'd finally get over the taciturn Sebastien, who had little interest in anything. Celine was fun and outgoing. She needed someone who was more like her, and Sam certainly had a lot of energy.

She also had a feeling that Berenice was charmed by Ben. Of course she was. He was just her type.

The later it got, the drunker they became, and Clémence realized that they had missed the last Métro.

Ben was quite drunk at that point, and Clémence was afraid that he'd fall over on the side of the street and that she would have to lug him home in a taxi and help him into the building.

Luckily, Sam lived a block away and put him up for the night. Rose took a cab because she was going in a different direction. The rest of the girls split a cab.

"I'm going to a tapas bar with Sam next Friday night," Celine said.

"That's sure to make Seb jealous," Clémence said, but she slapped a hand over her mouth when she realized that Berenice wasn't supposed to know about Celine's infatuation. "Sorry! The alcohol made me say it."

"Seb?" Berenice turned to Celine. "My brother Seb?"

Celine shook her head. "All right, fine. I had a crush on Seb for a while, but he doesn't seem interested."

Berenice chuckled a little. "Don't take it personally. He doesn't show interest in anybody. I don't even know what he's up to half the time."

"Please don't tell him," Celine groaned. "It's so embarrassing."

"I won't, I promise. Girl code."

"Forget him," Clémence said.

"It was so fun tonight," Celine said when Berenice was dropped off first. "We should hang out more often!"

Clémence was next to be dropped off. She was glad to have rounded up a group of friends together. She had always been friends with Berenice and Celine, but separately. Now perhaps they could hang out together outside of work more often.

When she got home, it was close to 2:30 a.m. No way was she going to wake up on time to go into work the next morning to help the bakers in the kitchen. Celine had a lunch shift, and it was Berenice's day off. And Ben... she didn't know what he did with his days except write in his little room.

When she went inside the iron doors of her building, she noticed that the door to la gardienne's apartment was slightly open. A small light was on inside, and it was moving—a flashlight! At the sound of the iron door clicking to a close, the flashlight went off.

Clémence thought about calling the police. There was the chance it was that silly inspector in there, but why would he do it in secrecy? It had to be the killer, looking for something.

Clémence waited. Sure enough, after a few minutes, the flashlight came back on. Whoever it was kept searching. Then the door opened. A tall figure dressed all in black came out. Clémence hid around the entrance to her building. When she heard the front door close, she went outside to take a peek at who it could be.

As soon as she opened the door and took a step outside, she felt a blow to her head, and then she was falling, falling to the ground.

Chapter 15

Sirens sounded in the distance. Clémence opened one eye and then the other. Arthur's face was inches away. Was he the one who had hit her? A hot flash of anger went through her, but she was too tired.

Her eyes were closed again, and she dreamed of black cats, drunk poets, and killers dressed like shadows.

When she woke up, she was in a hospital room. A doctor stood over her.

"No concussion," he said. "You're very lucky, young lady. You could've had permanent brain damage, too."

Brain damage? Clémence sat up. She had a headache that was worse than the jet-lag headache she'd just gotten over. It was more like a hangover headache. She had been drinking after all—and someone had hit her...

"You'll experience some headaches and minor dizziness that will last for the next three or four days," the doctor said.

"What happened?" she asked.

"Last night, I came home and found you lying on the street."

Clémence was surprised to see Arthur sitting calmly in a corner of the room.

"You!" Clémence exclaimed. "Are you the killer?"

"The killer? What?" Arthur looked offended.

Clémence explained what she remembered, that she had caught a glimpse of someone coming out of la gardienne's apartment dressed in all black. It was probably the same person who'd hit her.

"You think I'm the killer?" Arthur spat out. "If it wasn't for me, who knows what would've happened to you!"

"What were you doing coming home so late?" Clémence asked.

"I could ask you the same thing," Arthur said. "I was out."

"How can you prove that you're not the killer?"

"Look, if you must know, I had a friend with me."

Clémence leaned back. She raised an eyebrow. "One of your many girlfriends?"

"She's a friend," Arthur shot back. "So I have a witness. We found you lying on the ground in the middle of the sidewalk, and we immediately called the police."

"And you stayed here all night?" Clémence asked.

"Yes," he said, less defensive this time.

"You didn't call my parents, did you?"

"Not yet."

"Please don't," she said. "I don't want them to worry."

"Well, don't you think they have a right to be worried?"

Cyril came in through the door.

"Not you too," Clémence groaned.

"Nice to see you too," Cyril said, a little too cheerfully.

"Have you been listening the whole time?" asked Clémence.

"Yes. And this figure in black you saw—did you notice anything else?"

"No," Clémence muttered. "I wonder what he or she was looking for."

"The place was a mess," Cyril said. "The person had been looking through papers looking for documents."

"So la gardienne still has something on this killer?" Clémence wondered out loud.

"We have reason to believe that la gardienne had been opening the tenants' mail and resealing them,"

Cyril said. "She was looking through the tenants' mail for months to obtain their private information in order to blackmail them. We found a short note on her desk threatening someone else for twenty thousand euros."

"She had been blackmailing my father," Arthur said. "Yesterday night, I confronted my father, and he said that he had indeed been blackmailed."

"Then she was conveniently killed," Cyril said.

Arthur turned to him with a stern look. "It wasn't my father. I already told you where he was that night. He's a cheater but not a killer."

"Who else has she been blackmailing?" Clémence asked.

"Nobody we know of," Cyril said. "It could be a number of people. We found a bag containing seventy-six thousand euros so far under her bed. All cash."

"Oh my God," Clémence exclaimed.

"What about your parents?" Cyril asked. "Maybe la gardienne has tried to get money from them."

"I don't think so," Clémence said. "They have nothing to hide. I would know otherwise."

He narrowed his eyes at her. "Isn't it a little suspicious that they left for Asia?"

"No, that can't be. It's just a coincidence. Otherwise, they would tell me. I talk to them all the time, and they never sounded worried. They're having the time of their lives opening new Damour stores in Asia. Business is going really well for our company."

Cyril squinted. "Okay. Maybe." Cyril held out two plastic bags with a sheet of paper inside each one. "This is the note that Monsieur Dubois received. She'd been writing similar notes too. This is the one that la gardienne was working on before she was killed."

40,000 or the cat's out of the bag.

The writing was clumsy and shaky, probably written with a left hand to disguise it, but Clémence recognized something familiar about it.

"It's Lara's writing!" she exclaimed. "I recognize the *a*. The loop in her cursive goes halfway down."

"*C'est vrai?*" Arthur peered at the note. "How do you know?"

"She wrote her name and number down for me when I said I was interested in her cleaning services."

"The handwriting on the two notes are different," Cyril said. "Although both are incredibly shaky looking."

"Maybe Lara helped her with the first letter, and she did the other one herself," Clémence said. "Where is Lara now?"

"If I'm not mistaken," Arthur said, "she's working at the hair salon on Rue Saint-Didier."

Clémence slowly got out of bed so her head wouldn't spin as much. She was still wearing her clothes from last night, which smelled of booze and cigarette smoke.

"Where's my purse?"

Arthur got it for her. It was hanging from the back of the door.

"Hold on now," Cyril said. "This is still my investigation."

Clémence gave him a look. "I just helped you out big time. Lara is connected to this whole scheme. Let's go get her."

Chapter 16

The inspector was a horrible driver. He almost ran over three pedestrians on two separate occasions on the way to the hair salon. She'd felt safer riding on the back of a motorcycle four months earlier in Phnom Penh, Cambodia.

Several policemen were already standing outside the hair salon when they got there. Cyril had called them in case he needed to arrest Lara, but he would give them the go-ahead after he talked to her.

Cyril, Clémence, and Arthur went inside the salon, where two women and a man were in the middle of getting their hair cut or colored.

"Lara Silva?" Cyril glanced at the brunette who was washing a client's hair.

"That's not her," Clémence said. She suppressed the instinct to groan. He was supposed to know that Lara was the cleaner.

Lara was sweeping in one corner. Her plum lipstick was freshly applied on her lips, and there were bags under her eyes. Had she been crying recently?

"We'd like to speak to you in private," Clémence said firmly.

Lara's boss, a woman in her late forties with cat-eye glasses, demanded to know what was going on. After Cyril told her that he needed to speak to Lara and that he was an inspector, she let them use her office in the back of the salon.

Lara noticed Arthur glaring at Lara, who sat down and seemed to deflate in a chair. Cyril began right away.

"We know you're involved with la gardienne's blackmailing scheme."

At first, Lara remained stone faced, but her cheeks turned red. Tears welled up in her eyes.

"What were you doing, writing a ransom note to Monsieur Dubois?"

Lara shook her head as if she didn't want to hear anything further.

"Come on, Lara," Arthur said. "You did enough to our family. You owe it to us to tell us."

"All right," Lara sobbed. "Fine, I'll tell you." She took a tissue from the desk and blew her nose. "It was la gardienne's idea that I seduce Monsieur Dubois. Her plan was to catch us and then blackmail him by threatening to tell his wife. Then she promised to split the blackmail money with me."

Clémence heard Arthur take a deep breath, but he stayed silent.

"So it was successful, then," Clémence said.

Lara nodded. "She got the money from Dubois that afternoon, and so I went over in the evening, and she gave me my money."

"Then why were you so upset?" asked Clémence. "You went upstairs and shared a drink with your neighbor Ben. Shouldn't you have been happy?"

"Upset? Well. The truth is, I'd come to care for Monsieur Dubois." Lara couldn't look Arthur in the eye. "I thought he cared for me too, but after he gave the money to la gardienne, he wanted nothing to do with me even though he didn't know I was in on her scheme. He really didn't want to be caught even though he was always complaining about his wife and telling me how happy he was with me. I didn't expect his rejection to sting so much, but it did. I needed a drink when I went home, but I didn't have any wine left, and the stores were closed because it was late. I thought Ben might be able to comfort me, but he was quite dull. He kept chatting, and I waited for him to make a move, but he never did, so I left."

"So who killed la gardienne?" Cyril asked.

"I don't know," Lara said. "She was bragging about getting some money from some other tenants that she'd blackmailed and that she was about to hit a jackpot with someone new, but she didn't give me the details. When I heard the news the next day, I'd assumed that one of her blackmail victims had killed her. I didn't want to get involved, of course, so I didn't tell about Dubois."

"My father didn't do it," Arthur said. "For the last time. He was so drunk after dinner that he fell asleep in the living room, and we left him there."

"I didn't think he did," Lara softly. "He's not the type to do something like that."

"But the type to cheat on his wife," Arthur muttered. "With some cheap—"

"Okay," Clémence interjected. She steered the interrogation back on track. "Any idea who the other victims were? What kind of dirt did she have? Did she make any other plans to trap tenants into uncompromising situations like with you and Dubois?"

"I don't know. She said she wanted to get a couple in their fifties in the other building because they were always playing their music too loud. I'm not sure what happened. She really wanted to get back at the Dubois family because she hated them. The children, I agree, are nasty."

"Hey!" Arthur interjected.

"It's true," Lara spat back. "They threw condom water balloons at her door, and your mother would claim that they're innocent when they're not."

"*Calmez-vous*," Cyril said. "Calm down. Who else did she have a vendetta against?"

"She also didn't like this French student who lives on the roof. He'd leave his hair in the shower and didn't flush the public toilet sometimes."

"You think she'd blackmail him for money too?" Clémence asked.

"I don't know," she said. "The student probably doesn't have much money. La gardienne doesn't tell me everything. Like I said, I was only involved in the Dubois situation."

Cyril's face fell. Clémence knew it was because they were back at square one. It could be a number of people. Could it even be Madame Dubois? She didn't want to suggest this out loud to Arthur. He looked upset enough.

Arthur stood up and glowered at Lara with extreme hatred. "You're fired, you hear? I want you out of that room by tomorrow. I don't care where you go. Just get out."

He stormed out, and Lara began crying.

Chapter 17

"So that's the story so far," Clémence said.

She told Sebastien all that had happened. It had been three days, and they still had not found the killer. Cyril and his team had gone around interrogating the tenants again. He might've uncovered more blackmail cases, details he refused to tell her, but as far as Clémence knew, no one had been arrested.

"What do you guys think? Is there something I'm missing?"

"No clue," Sebastien said.

"Well, it's something to do with a document—a clue that the killer didn't want us to have that he or she thought was still in la gardienne's apartment."

"But then again, you didn't know what was there to begin with, so it's hard to say what's missing, isn't it?" Sebastien poured cream into a piping bag.

"Exactly," Clémence said. "I think we've hit a wall."

Sebastien was putting the cream on the flat ends of the macaron shells. Each one was topped with another shell to make the macaron sandwich. He had made the green-tea flavor.

"Try it." He gave one to Clémence.

"Perfect." Clémence smiled. "Can you make some more? Hmm. Really delicious."

"Perfect, huh?" Sebastien grinned. "It only took a dozen tries."

"Worth the effort, don't you think?" Clémence said. "I love my job."

"So you're pretty careful these days, right?" Sebastien asked her. "I mean, someone in your building almost gave you a concussion. Aren't you afraid?"

"Nah. I know a little self-defense. I'm not afraid. I just can't be so careless."

"If you're ever going home alone late at night, you have to watch out."

"Thanks, Sebastien."

Seb was a caring guy beneath the façade of indifference. She was glad to have him as a friend. If Celine could see this side of him, she'd fall even harder in love. Lately, she'd been passing the time with Sam, so maybe she was over Seb already.

Berenice came in to start her shift. She was glowing more than usual.

"Hey, how did things go with Ben?" Clémence asked her.

"We had a good time yesterday night," she said. "We picnicked at the Pont des Art. Then we're supposed to meet up for a casual drink tomorrow. But no biggie. We're just hanging out."

Clémence knew the look on her friend's face. One part mischief and one part naiveté. She was falling fast, but Berenice fell out of love just as often.

"Remember," Seb said. "If he asks you to go home, say no. That's guy code for one thing."

Berenice rolled her eyes. "Oh, we're well aware of what guys want. It's what girls want that guys are oblivious to."

"Just be careful," Seb warned.

Clémence and Berenice laughed. Sometimes, she didn't know what to make of him. It was as if his personality changed every day. Today, Seb played the part of the concerned father.

Clémence went home after lunch to let the cleaner, Magda, in. This was the first time she'd met the middle-aged cleaner, and she came in with her bag of supplies and the day's mail: some bills for Clémence's parents, a postcard from her mom from when she was in Tokyo, and a letter addressed to her. It was an invoice from the dentist that she would submit to her insurance.

In the kitchen, she had a cup of tea and read the postcard. Her mom had etched out an anecdote about getting lost on the train. Apparently, they had taken the express by mistake, and they ended up missing their stop. Then they took the wrong train again in the opposite direction. It wasn't a classic anecdote, but her mother was easily amused by most things.

She opened up the invoice next, and her eyes widened in shock at the amount that was billed to her. She was supposed to be charged for a checkup, not getting her wisdom teeth pulled. Although Clémence's family was wealthy now, they had grown up very much middle class, where things like money did matter a great deal.

After she finished her tea, she went downstairs right away to sort out the matter.

"I'll be right back, Magda!"

"*Oui, madame.*"

Miffy barked a farewell as well.

It was past 2:00 p.m., but the dentist seemed to be closed. The little plaque on the door said they were closed between 12:45 p.m. and 2:30 p.m. for lunch. Lunch was a proper affair in France. It wasn't unusual for certain offices and restaurants to be closed for extended periods of time.

She was about to go back upstairs when she heard footsteps coming up from the main floor. It was the dentist, Phillipe Rousseau, who grinned at the sight of her.

"Can I help you with something?" he asked.

"*Bonjour, monsieur.* I think your secretary made a small error with my invoice."

"Oh?"

She showed him the paper. "I only had a cleaning. My wisdom teeth were pulled a long time ago."

Phillipe chuckled in embarrassment.

"I'm so sorry. Suzanne must've mixed up the accounts. I can help you get that sorted right away."

"I didn't mean to bother you during your lunchtime," Clémence said. "I didn't know your hours."

Phillipe unlocked the door, still smiling. "No problem. We can get this fixed in a minute."

They went in, and he took off his coat and threw it on a chair in the waiting room. Then he began to type on the receptionist's computer.

Clémence never knew his coat was Burberry until she saw the label. It was an olive-colored coat that she didn't typically associate with the brand.

The buttons were like the wooden one Miffy had chewed on, except one on the bottom of the coat was a shade darker than the rest—a replacement button.

"Is anything the matter?"

Phillipe was staring at her.

Clémence looked up at him. "No. I was just—admiring your jacket. I'd like to buy my father one."

"Ah, yes."

Phillipe stepped around and held up the jacket. "It's quite nice, isn't it? I've had it for five or six years now, and it's still as good as new."

Except for the button. But it could've meant anything. She didn't even have proof that Miffy took the button from inside la gardienne's apartment, and if she did, so what? She already knew that Phillipe had been inside her house to help her check her teeth, as he'd already explained to her. It didn't mean that he was the killer.

But the way he was blocking her from the door made Clémence uncomfortable. And the clouded look in his dark eyes. She took a step and Phillipe blocked her.

"All right." His voice became sharp. "What do you know?"

"What?"

"Don't play dumb, Damour. I know you've been snooping around. You've got a head injury or something?"

Phillipe chuckled.

Clémence's hands turned into fists.

"So it was you! You were the one who hit me!"

Phillipe laughed. "Serves you right for getting into my business."

"But why?" Clémence tried to stall for time.

"Why? Oh, that gardienne. I hate snoops. She opened my mail. Knew that a former client was taking me to court for charging her for a surgery I didn't perform."

"So you committed dental fraud?"

"Yes. I needed some extra money for my family. We have five kids. Paris is not a cheap place to live, you know, at least for the working class."

He glanced at her as if she should be apologizing for being rich.

"The whole thing could've been cast aside if it wasn't for her," he said. "I would've just paid the settlement—that is, if they could even prove that I committed dental fraud. I've done this for years, but that had been the only time that I'd been caught. It all would've gone away if it wasn't for la gardienne. She was threatening to ruin my reputation, have my license pulled, tell each of my clients who passed through the door what I've been accused of doing. She wanted a one-hundred-thousand-euro payout! Well, I couldn't have that now, could I? What if she kept pumping me for money for the rest of my life? I had a lot to lose."

"So you just killed her?"

"Well, I hadn't planned on it. I was just going to talk some sense into her, give her some free dental care, but no. She wouldn't budge. So I hit her, and she never got up. That's not killing."

"It is if she's dead," Clémence said.

Phillipe chuckled again. His eyes shone, looking at her as if she was prey.

"Well, if I'm already a killer, then I might as well continue."

He lunged at her, but Clémence screamed and jerked away. "You can't do this! Help!"

He put a hand over her mouth. "No one's in this office for the next half hour. No one's on the floor above either, so they won't hear your screams. I can do whatever I want with you at this point."

Chapter 18

He began to choke her from behind.

Clémence quickly gathered all her strength and knocked her head back to butt him in the forehead, then jabbed him in the gut with an elbow. She quickly spun around and kicked him hard in the groin.

She'd learned a little self-defense from a friend when she was in Morocco.

"Ow!" He stumbled, clutching his crotch area.

Clémence escaped out the door, shouting, "Au secours! Au secours! Help! Help!"

Clémence ran outside and found some construction workers restoring the façade of a building two doors down. She explained that the dentist had attacked her. When Phillipe ran out after her, she pointed him out to them, and they held him down until the police came and arrested him.

The street was, once again, chaos. Police cars blocked one of the lanes while drivers slowed down to see what was going on. The building's residents and pedestrians formed a crowd, many shocked to witness their local dentist handcuffed and shoved into the back of a police car.

When Cyril arrived on the scene, Clémence was the one smiling smugly this time. "My head's pounding, my arm hurts, and I almost got killed, but at least somebody got the job done."

He rolled his eyes. "Oh, don't be so dramatic, Damour."

"You're welcome," she retorted.

"I don't know how you did it, but I'm sure it was all luck."

His words were biting, but the sour expression on his face made her laugh out loud.

He sighed. "You might as well come with me to the station. I need your statement."

The grin wouldn't come off her face. Her heart was still pounding and her body ached, but she couldn't think of anything more satisfying than seeing a killer captured and a sardonic inspector defeated.

Celine, Berenice, and Sebastien came around to Clémence's place after she returned from the police station. They wanted to make sure that she was all right. Sebastien had even brought a box of the macarons that they'd created together. Ben came downstairs as well when Clémence texted him. He had a bottle of wine in hand. Wine was Ben's solution to life's problems.

Clémence shook her head. "A murderous dentist. Who would've thought? He could've just been a fraudulent dentist with a revoked license instead of a murderer."

She felt sorry for Phillipe's kids. Imagine having a psychopathic murderer and con artist for a father.

"You're such a badass," Berenice exclaimed. "Beating him down like that."

They had gathered in her living room, drinking wine in the middle of the afternoon.

"Don't tell my parents, guys," Clémence said. "I don't want them to worry and come home early because of this small incident."

"You could've been dead." Sebastien frowned. "It's no small incident."

"Stop being so pessimistic," Berenice said.

"She could've had another concussion."

"True." Berenice examined Clémence. "But she looks fine. She's alive and well, and she helped solve the case. It's all behind her now."

"That inspector should be kissing your ass," Ben said in his heavily accented French.

"He's grateful," Clémence said. "I think. But he'll never admit it. And he'll never apologize for accusing me of being the murderer either."

"Let's toast to Clémence," said Ben. He raised his glass and the others did the same. "To Clémence's kicking a murderer's ass. You've got eight lives left."

They laughed and clinked glasses, making sure to look each other in the eyes as they did. If they didn't hold eye contact while clinking glasses, a French superstition stipulated that they would have seven years of bad sex.

Their celebration was interrupted by the doorbell. Usually guests had to buzz from downstairs to get into the building. Clémence wondered if it was just Magda who'd forgotten something since she had just left. Who else could it be?

Clémence must've been on edge from the afternoon's incident because she was apprehensive about answering the door. Sebastien noticed and offered to come with her.

There was no one there when she looked through the peephole. She stepped back. Slowly, Sebastien opened the door.

They were both surprised to find a bouquet of roses on the floor. An elegant card in a cream envelope simply said, "To Clémence" in neat handwriting.

"Who's it from?" Berenice and the others approached from behind.

Clémence lit up at the sight of the lavish bouquet. She bent down and smelled them. The red and pink roses were gorgeous.

"A secret admirer?" Sebastien arched an eyebrow.

"I don't know," she said, the grin returning to her face. "I guess it's another mystery to be solved."

Recipes

French macarons have a reputation for being difficult to make. While it may be true that it can be a challenge for professional bakers to get the shells looking perfect, you can still make delicious macarons to enjoy at home. Don't worry if the shells are cracked or come out a little darker in some areas. They'll still taste just as good.

A perfect macaron will have a firm shell with a moist interior. It shouldn't be too chewy but melt-in-your-mouth light.

Here are some simplified macaron recipes (tradition and unique flavors) that Clémence and her friends—as well as la gardienne—have enjoyed in the book.

Recipe 1

Pistachio Macarons with Oreo Cream Filling

Makes about 15-18 sandwiches

Macaron Shells:

- 1 1/4 cups icing sugar
- 1 1/4 cups ground almonds (or almond meal/ almond flour)
- 1 ounce unsalted blanched pistachios
- 4 egg whites
- 1/4 cup baker's sugar/caster sugar

Oreo Cream Filling:

- 1 cup icing sugar, sieved
- 3/4 cup butter, softened
- Pinch of salt
- 5 Oreo cookies, crumbled finely (including cream filling)

For shells:

Preheat oven to 300° F. Line a baking tray.

In a bowl, mix the pistachios and almonds. Sift in the icing sugar.

In another bowl, whisk the egg whites until stiff, then add one tablespoon of baker's sugar. Continue to whisk on high speed while adding remaining sugar.

Stir almond mixture into the egg whites and gently mix with a spatula. Add green food coloring.

Put mixture into a pastry bag with a round nozzle. Pipe one-inch circles onto the baking tray, making sure there is enough space between each (one inch apart).

Tap the tray on a table to remove any air bubbles and set the macarons aside for 30 minutes. This allows a crust to form on the macarons. Then bake in the oven for 14 minutes.

Test to see if your shells are ready by lightly pressing the top. If they are still soft and moving, they are not ready yet.

Oreo cream filling:

Beat icing sugar, butter, and salt with electric beater until smooth. Mix in crumbled cookies.

Assembly:

Take one macaron and pipe/spread the filling on the flat part, then add a second macaron on top. Repeat until no macarons are left.

You can eat them on the same day, but if you can resist, refrigerate and wait until the next day. They will taste better.

Recipe 2

Lychee Macarons with Raspberry Buttercream

Makes about 15 sandwiches

Macaron Shells:
- 1 cup ground almonds, sifted (or almond meal/almond flour)
- 1/2 cup powdered sugar, heaped and sifted
- 2 egg whites
- 5 tbsp granulated sugar
- 1 can lychees, drained and sliced

Raspberry Buttercream:
- 2/3 cup raspberries
- 3/4 cup butter, softened
- 1 1/4 cups powdered sugar, sifted

For shells:

Preheat oven to 280° F. Line a baking tray. Beat egg whites in a large mixing bowl with an electric beater for one minute. Add in granulated sugar. After another minute, add food coloring. Beat until you can hold the bowl upside down and the egg mixture does not move, about 5 to 7 minutes.

Fold in almonds and powdered sugar with a flexible spatula. Scrape the sides of the bowl and move the mixture to the middle. Do this until everything is mixed well.

Pour the batter into a piping bag. Pipe into one-inch circles, leaving one inch between each. Should be around thirty circles.

Leave shells to dry for 30 minutes. Bake for 15 minutes, rotating the tray halfway through baking time.

When finished baking, let shells cool completely before attempting to remove them from the tray. If the shells are cracked, they will still be delicious.

For cream:

Mix butter in a bowl on medium high until soft and fluffy.

In a saucepan, put the raspberries in with a splash of water and heat on low for 10 minutes. Drain raspberries and push through a strainer to remove the seeds. Let raspberries cool before adding the butter. Mix together.

Add powdered sugar in three parts. You may add additional powdered sugar to thicken the buttercream.

Assembly:

Turn macaron shells on their backs. Fill a piping bag with the buttercream and pipe small mounds of cream onto every other shell. Place a small cut piece of lychee on the cream before topping with the second shell.

Recipe 3

Classic Chocolate Macarons with Chocolate Ganache

Makes about 25 sandwiches

Macaron Shells:

- 1 cup ground almonds (or almond meal/almond flour)
- 2 cups powdered sugar
- 3 large egg whites, room temperature
- 3 tbsp natural unsweetened cocoa powder
- 1/4 tsp salt
- 3 tbsp granulated sugar
- Pinch cream of tartar

Chocolate Ganache:

- 4 ounces bittersweet chocolate, finely chopped
- 1/2 cup heavy cream
- 2 tbsp unsalted butter, room temperature, cubed

For shells:

Preheat oven to 350° F. Arrange a rack in the middle. Line two baking sheets with parchment paper.

Put the powdered sugar, almond flour, cocoa powder, and salt in a food processor and pulse several times to aerate. Process until fine and combined, around 30 seconds. Sift through a flour sifter into a large bowl.

In a clean bowl, beat egg whites with an electric mixer on medium speed until opaque and foamy, around 30 seconds. Add the cream of tartar and increase the speed to medium high. Beat until the egg whites are white in color and continue for another minute. Slowly add in granulated sugar and continue beating until sugar is combined, the peaks are stiff, and the whites are shiny, around one minute. Don't over-whip.

Fold dry mixture into the egg white mix in four batches, using a rubber spatula. The meringue will deflate. Stop folding when there are no traces of egg whites and it looks like cake batter. Don't over-mix.

Transfer batter into a pastry bag. Pipe one-inch circles on the baking sheets, one inch apart. There should be 25 per tray. Bang the trays on your work surface. Leave the trays at room temperature for

30 minutes to dry the shells. This will ensure even cooking.

Bake the shells one tray at a time for 14 minutes each. Rotate the sheet in the middle of the cooking time. Let it cool completely.

For ganache:

Place the chopped chocolate in a large bowl.

In a small saucepan over medium heat, warm the cream until it starts to boil. Stir in the chocolate. Let it sit for one minute. Add butter and stir until smooth. Chill in the fridge until thick and spreadable, around 30 minutes.

Assembly:

Pipe or scoop about a teaspoon of the ganache to the flat surface of one shell. Top with another shell and press gently. Refrigerate, covered, for at least 24 hours.

Recipe 4

Matcha Green Tea Macarons with Matcha Buttercream

Makes over 20 sandwiches

For shells:
- 1 1/2 cups almond powder
- 1 cup powdered sugar
- 5 egg whites
- 1 tsp matcha powder
- 1/2 cup granulated sugar
- 2 tsp vanilla extract
- 1/2 tsp green food coloring (optional)

For the buttercream:
- 1 cup butter, room temperature
- 2/3 cup icing sugar
- 2 tsp vanilla extract
- 4 tbsp whipping cream
- 4 tbsp matcha powder

For shells:

Preheat oven at 300° F. For best possible results, grind almond powder, powdered sugar and matcha powder together for a minute to ensure that the almonds are evenly dispersed with the sugar. Sift it into a bowl. (If there are larger pieces left, grind them and sift them again.)

In another bowl, combine egg whites, sugar, and vanilla and beat for around three minutes until the egg whites are frothy. Turn up speed to medium high and beat for another three minutes. You should have soft peaks by now. Turn speed up to high and beat for another three minutes. This will give you stiff, dry peaks. Add food coloring and beat on high for another minute. Pour all your almond mixture in at once. Fold everything with a plastic spatula.

Pour it into a piping bag and pipe onto a lined baking tray in one-inch circles, one inch apart. Once finished, tap against table or counter to dislodge air bubbles. Set it aside for 30 minutes to up to one and a half hours to dry out shells. Bake for about 15 to 20 minutes.

For the buttercream:

Cream the butter until light and fluffy, around 4 minutes. Add in the rest of the ingredients and beat for another 4 minutes.

For assembly:

Pipe the buttercream on one shell and sandwich them together. Put the macarons in the fridge for 24 hours before eating. Eat them at room temperature.

Recipe 5:

Black Sesame Macarons with Red Bean Filling

Makes 15-20 sandwiches

Macaron Shells:

- 1 1/2 cups almond flour
- 1 1/2 tbsp black sesame powder (found at Asian specialty supermarkets)
- 1 3/4 cups powdered sugar
- 5 egg whites
- 1/3 cup granulated sugar
- 1/2 tsp salt
- 1 tsp vanilla extract

Filling:

- Sweetened red bean paste

For Shells:

Preheat oven to 300° F. Line three trays with parchment paper. Grind almond flour and black sesame powder for 30 seconds in a food processor. Sift this and powdered sugar together in a bowl and set aside.

Combine egg whites, sugar, and salt. Mix with an electric mixer on medium for 3 minutes. Increase speed to medium-high and whip for another 3 minutes. Go to high and whip for another 3 minutes. Add vanilla and beat for one more minute on high.

Add dry ingredients. Mix with spatula until batter melts back down in 20 seconds. Transfer to a piping bag.

Pipe one-inch circles on your trays, leaving one inch between them. Bang the tray on your work surface to let air bubbles out. Let the macarons sit for 30 minutes to an hour.

Bake for 18 minutes. Let cool completely. The shells should be a light beige color with hints of black sesames.

Assembly:

Roll a teaspoon's worth of red bean paste into a ball. Press flat until it matches the size of a shell. Place the flattened paste on the flat surface of one shell. Top with another shell. Since the paste is firm, be careful when you press the shell, as you might accidentally crush them.

About the Author

*H*arper Lin lives in Kingston, Ontario with her husband, daughter, and Pomeranian puppy. The Patisserie Mysteries draws from Harper's own experiences of living in Paris in her twenties. When she's not reading or writing mysteries, she is hiking, in yoga class, or spending time with her friends and family. She's currently working on more cozy mysteries.

www.harperlin.com

Made in the USA
Columbia, SC
22 September 2020